Desolation Point

All is not well with the Somerset Nuclear Electric power station at Desolation Point. It is being picketed by a women's pressure group, and Liam, the infant son of one of the station's employees, has died of leukæmia, which the women claim was caused by the station.

Then Michael Hempstead, a senior engineer at the station, becomes involved with Sarah Brierly, one of the group's organizers, and things begin to happen.

A colleague of Michael's is found dead. Accident or murder? There is a radiation leak. Accident or sabotage? A more obvious attempt at sabotage is made by Liam's father, deranged by grief. There is another violent death.

These events are accompanied by a vitriolic media campaign carried out by a suspiciously well-informed local newspaper, and Michael's boss becomes convinced that Sarah is using information gleaned from Michael to help orchestrate this campaign—something which Michael refuses to believe.

Then Michael himself is attacked and nearly killed and the station is hit by an altogether more serious 'mishap'.

Something very sinister is going on at Desolation Point, and the stakes are sky high.

ANDREW PUCKETT

Desolation Point

THE CRIME CLUB
An Imprint of HarperCollins *Publishers*

First published in Great Britain in 1993
by The Crime Club, an imprint of
HarperCollins Publishers, 77–85 Fulham Palace Road,
Hammersmith, London W6 8JB

9 8 7 6 5 4 3 2 1

A catalogue record for this book is
available from the British Library.

ISBN 0 00 232443 1

Photoset in Linotron Baskerville by
Rowland Phototypesetting Ltd
Bury St Edmunds, Suffolk
Printed and bound in Great Britain by
HarperCollins Book Manufacturing, Glasgow.

For Holly
and her mother

Acknowledgement

I would like to thank Bill Gray and Colin Gray for their expert professional advice.

CHAPTER 1

THIS IS MY SON LIAM

Murdered by Somerset Nuclear Electric

As soon as I saw the placard, a blow-up of Liam's face attached, I knew the worst must have happened. Jane didn't move, just stood there holding it, her own face a mixture of loathing and contempt. She was flanked by two of the Women, one of them, I dimly realized, the Gorgeous One. A TV cameraman was setting up.

There was no point in trying to say anything. I stopped at the gate, showed my pass to the security guard, then drove into the station.

Maybe it was my imagination, but the overcast day gave the sea a dirty, sullen hue, and the stark grey bulk of the Reactor Building, rearing into the sky, seemed to jar against both of them. I parked the Midget, took the lift up to the sixth floor and went straight to David's office.

'Oh, good afternoon,' he said. 'I've been trying to phone you.'

'Sorry.' I glanced at the wall clock behind him. It was only ten past, not that bad. 'David, I saw Jane at the gate . . .'

'Liam died yesterday,' he said flatly, reaching for his pack of cigarettes and lighting one.

'Have you spoken to Steve?' I asked. Steve was Liam's father and an employee of the station.

'I tried ringing last night when I heard, and again this morning.' He blew smoke. 'Engaged both times. Left off the hook, I shouldn't wonder.'

As he spoke, his own phone rang. He picked it up.

'Rossily . . .'

David Rossily, my boss. Welsh, as was everything about him. A hard, compact little man bursting with energy. Intense dark features: hair, eyes, moustache against a pale, slightly gaunt face, and with a fearsome reputation for philandering . . .

'That was Sir,' he said, replacing the phone. 'He's called an emergency Heads of Departments meeting at ten in the board room.'

'What about?'

'This whole mess, I should imagine.'

'Anything I should know?'

He shook his head. 'Just be there. On time, if possible.'

'OK, OK. David, is there anything we can do?'

'For Steve and Jane, you mean? I've been asking myself that question all night, and the answer is no. Nothing that won't be thrown back into our faces.'

Steve Holford had been the best of the men in my gang. Twenty-five, fair-haired and ruddy-faced, he was always cheerful, enjoying his work. Then, eighteen months earlier, leukæmia had been diagnosed in his two-year-old son, Liam. At first he and Jane had been positive, determined to fight. Liam was treated and the disease went into remission. We all hoped and some of us prayed. Then, three months before, he had relapsed, and shortly afterwards Jane had been approached by WANT, Women Against Nuclear Technology, who had persuaded her that radiation from the station had affected Steve's sperm, so that Liam had been doomed from the moment he was conceived. WANT had put up the money for Steve and Jane to sue Somerset Nuclear Electric for negligence, and had then picketed the station. Steve had been suspended, at his own request, on full pay, and had more or less cut himself off from his colleagues.

*

I made my way back to my own office, but was intercepted by Rod Ashcott, another of my gang.

'Water supply's dropping on number three oil cooler, Michael, and the oil temperature's going up.'

'Can't you or Darren fix it?'

'Darren doesn't like the look of it. Thought you ought to have a look.'

'Oh, all right.'

I followed him into the lift. As it went down he said, 'Shitty about Steve's little boy, eh?'

'Yeah,' I said shortly. The lift doors opened and we were enveloped by the noise of the turbines. We put on hard hats and adjusted the ear muffles.

It took half an hour to fix the oil cooler, by which time it was a quarter to ten and my hands were covered in oil. I hurried to the Gents', still feeling slightly resentful that they hadn't been able to sort it out themselves. Steve would have . . .

I got the worst of the muck off and was reaching for a paper towel when my eye was caught by the angle of my head in the mirror, frozen for an instant like a still from a film.

Is that what people see? I wondered. Is that what the Gorgeous One sees?

An angular face with short brown hair and beard. An inoffensive enough face, so what makes it angular, I wonder? The cheekbones are the key to the flavour of any face, and mine . . .

The door threw open and Don Waterford strode in.

'Ooh, you are rather lovely, aren't you, ducky?'

Peter Broomfield came in after him. I took a paper towel and dried my hands.

'Just making sure I'm reasonably oil free. Are you going to the meeting?'

'Yeah. Any idea what it's about?'

'Liam Holford, I should think. You've heard, I imagine?'

'Yeah. Rough luck, that.'

Something in his voice made me quickly look at him. Although the expression on his strong, rather coarsely handsome face was sober, his bright blue eyes were glinting with . . . malice? He caught my own expression and went on hurriedly, 'Best thing for them, though. Steve and Jane, I mean. Best his suffering's over now.'

'You're a hard bastard, aren't you, Don? You don't give a toss.'

It was completely spontaneous, surprising me as much as him. His eyes blazed and he took a step towards me.

'You're not this station's conscience, Michael. Don't you tell me how I should feel about anything . . .'

With a sudden movement that made me flinch, he pulled a comb from his pocket, then, turning to the mirror, thrust it through his thick reddish hair.

I glared at him a moment to leave him in no doubt how I felt, then pushed past in front of him to the door. Peter's pale eyes in his pale, naked head avoided mine. Outside, I tried to calm down as I made my way to the board room.

Other than Sir (Edward Harper, Station Manager and Lord of All), the only people already there were his secretary, and James Westhay, the station's Administrator.

' 'Morning, Michael. Nice to see you so prompt.' He gave a sniff. 'Are the others on their way, d'you know?'

'Don and Peter are. And David, I believe.' I chose a seat a few removed from him.

'Good.' He paused, then said: 'Sad news about Liam Holford. I hope his parents will be allowed to grieve in peace now.'

'Yes,' I said, looking at him. For all his pomposity and vested interest, I could see that he was sincere. More sincere than Don, anyway.

Westhay was making sycophantic agreeing noises when the door opened and Dr Fitzpatrick, the station Medical Officer, came in.

''Morning, George,' said Sir. He was the only person in the station who called him by his Christian name. 'Take a seat.'

Sir was already flanked by his secretary and Westhay, who was hoping to appear powerful by proximity perhaps, so with a grunt, Fitzpatrick chose a chair at the opposite end of the table.

George Fitzpatrick was the epitome of the crusty country medic: short, plump, dressed in tweeds and with an irascible face under thinning, sandy hair. He was a good doctor, though.

'I hope this isn't going to take too long, Edward,' he rumbled. 'I have an Occupational Health Clinic in half an hour.'

'I think we may be able to let you get away before then, George.'

'Good.'

Don and Peter came in.

''Morning, Mr Harper,' Don said smartly, trying to ingratiate himself as usual. The trouble was, it seemed to work.

'Good morning to you, Don. Take a seat. And you, Peter.'

Don chose a seat on the other side of the table from me and said to Sir in a lower voice, 'Sad news about little Liam Holford.'

'Indeed it is,' said Sir. 'We were just saying the same thing.'

David arrived, accompanied by John Burton, our newest Department Head.

''Morning, David,' Sir said briskly. 'John. Find yourselves seats. Are we all here now?'

'Rhiannon was held up, Mr Harper,' John said as they sat next to me. 'She'll be along shortly.'

'Oh. Well, I think we'd better get started. I've called this meeting at such short notice because of the sad death yesterday of Liam Holford from leukæmia, and the subsequent inflammatory interview given by the leader of WANT last night on Western TV.'

Sir cut an imposing figure, tall, with a large, powerful head and iron grey hair, the fleshiness around his face and the slightly protruding stomach the only signs of his sedentary life.

'We will, of course, be sending a wreath to the funeral, and making a substantial donation to CLIC, the Cancer and Leukæmia in Childhood charity, but our immediate problem is: should we, considering the circumstances, send a representative to the funeral? And if so, who?' His hooded grey eyes seemed to take us all in.

'Not an easy question,' said David. 'And certainly not an enviable task for the representative.'

I said, 'Rhiannon was Liam's godparent, so she's probably in the best position to know.'

At that moment, there was a tap on the door and Rhiannon came in.

'I'm sorry I'm late, Mr Harper, I was—'

'That's quite all right, my dear, you couldn't have timed it better. Find yourself a seat.'

She walked quickly round the table and sat on the other side of me from David. She was wearing a filmy dress which suited her slender figure, and a delicate perfume. Obviously not expecting any practical work today.

'We were wondering whether we should send a representative to Liam Holford's funeral,' Sir said.

Rhiannon lifted her head.

'Probably not a good idea,' she replied in her clear voice. 'I was Liam's godmother. In the latter stages of his illness, his mother made it fairly plain that my visits were no longer welcome, so I suggest we send a wreath and leave it at last.'

'Thank you, Rhiannon. David, you wanted to say something?'

'I was wondering about the wisdom of sending a donation to CLIC. Might it not be construed by WANT and the media as a tacit admission of responsibility?'

'Oh, that's a bit cynical, surely, David,' said Don quickly. 'It would be a simple and sincere expression of our regret, our sympathy.'

'From us, yes,' said David, 'but—'

'I think I agree with you there, Don,' said Sir, overriding him. 'But we can take legal advice on it. I would like to turn now to the implications of Liam's death for Somerset Nuclear Electric. However distasteful this may seem, it has to be considered. Dr Fitzpatrick has to leave us shortly, so perhaps I could ask him now to outline, very briefly, the medical aspects of the case as they concern us. George.'

Fitzpatrick cleared his throat.

'Liam died from Acute Lymphoblastic Leukæmia, which is the most common leukæmia in childhood. Overall, there is nearly a ninety per cent cure rate now for childhood leukæmia, but Liam was one of the unlucky ten per cent. As we know, his parents, with the encouragement of WANT, are now in the process of preparing a writ against us for negligence.

'This stems from the legal action being taken by three sets of parents in Cumbria against the reprocessing plant at Sellafield. The parents in these cases are claiming that the father's sperm was affected before conception by radiation from the plant, thus causing the children to be born with a genetic predisposition to leukæmia. There has been some recent research which appears, superficially, to support this view.' He cleared his throat again, probably for effect.

'I've studied the medical evidence in the literature and in all the relevant research papers behind these cases, and it is my opinion, along with the majority of the medical profession, that it is most unlikely that radiation from Sella-field was responsible.'

He looked around at us, a slight sardonic expression around his lips. 'This is not to say, of course, that they won't be *found* responsible. However, on balance, I don't think they will, and I think it even more unlikely that the Holfords' case will succeed. In fact, I would imagine they'll drop it if and when the Sellafield cases fail. In other words, WANT are flying a kite, and not one that's of any benefit whatsoever to the Holfords.'

'Which doesn't stop the bad publicity it's bringing us for the moment,' said Sir. 'Are there any questions anyone wants to ask Dr Fitzpatrick?'

There was a general shaking of heads and Sir said, 'All right, George, you'd better get off to your clinic.'

And with another grunt, George did just that.

'Which brings us back to WANT and their attack on us last night on Western TV. While not accusing us outright of causing Liam's death, they certainly made a meal of it, and they did accuse us of being hypocrites. They said that our open house policy is a sham and that we only allow the public to see the things we want them to see. That cannot be allowed to pass unchallenged.' He looked round at us all again.

'As I said earlier, this is a highly distasteful matter, especially to those of us who know the Holfords, but the fact is that WANT are milking this tragedy for all it's worth. We must go on the offensive ourselves, or we're going to lose this propaganda battle.

'The question is, how . . . ?'

CHAPTER 2

Women Against Nuclear Technology, WANT, had been
formed when a section of the Greenham Common Women
had realized they'd become effectively redundant once the
cousins took the 'missles' back home. So, leaving their less
perceptive sisters behind, they'd spent some time reorganiz-
ing themselves, then looked around for a suitable nuclear
installation to picket.

Whether it was Liam's illness that made them pick on
Somerset Nuclear Electric rather than somewhere like
Sellafield, I don't know. Perhaps Sellafield was too big, too
far away from London. Perhaps it was the name of our
location on the coast—Desolation Point—that was the
attraction. It was certainly an unfortunate name from our
point of view.

Anyway, they'd arrived one morning some two months
before, about fifty of them, and set up their tents. More
had come since and there were now over a hundred.

They were peaceful and non-violent, not attempting to
break in or cause any damage. They were well-organized:
there was none of the squalor often associated with protest
groups. They canvassed the local towns and villages and
handed out leaflets to all the station's visitors. They'd given
interviews in the local press and on local television. Already,
several school parties had cancelled scheduled visits to us.

They'd used Liam's illness, certainly, but subtly until
now, so that they couldn't be accused of bad taste.

They were *there*, omnipresent, a silent reproof or a
damned nuisance, depending on your point of view.
Already, it seemed as though they'd been there for
ever.

*

'Well,' said Sir now, 'does anyone have any ideas? James—'
he turned to the Administrator—'any news about the docu-
mentary Pan European Films were making for us?'

'I went up to London last week, Mr Harper, and they
ran through the draft for me. I must say I was very im-
pressed with it. I think it could be a great help to us in this
situation.'

'Have Western TV said they'll screen it yet?'

'We have every reason to think they will, although they'll
want to see it themselves first. Western TV have always
treated us fairly.'

This was true, by and large. One of the local papers, the
Western Evening News, had been far worse, placing articles
about the station on the same page as medical reports on
Liam, linking the two in the public mind.

'When will it be ready?'

'About a month. Two at the outside.'

'A month or two is no use to us. We need something *now*.'

'I could try and chivvy them a bit.'

'Could we have something this week? Or next?'

'Er—to be honest, Mr Harper, I doubt it.'

'There is something else, Mr Harper,' said Don.

'Yes, Don?'

'However good the film turns out to be, however soon
we get it, we'll still be open to the accusation that it's a fix,
a whitewash.'

'You could be right, but there's not a great deal we can
do about it now, is there? We need something fresh.'

'As a matter of fact, I did have an idea, after seeing the
programme last night.'

'Well, let's hear it.'

'WANT has said that we're hypocrites, that we pretend
to be open when we're really hiding things. I suggest that
we invite them, publicly, to nominate a representative who
can spend as long as she likes going round the station—
escorted by one of us, of course—' he smiled, crinkling

the skin round his blue eyes—'but looking everywhere she pleases. Whatever they try to say about it afterwards, it will make a nonsense of their claim that we're hiding anything.'

Sir slowly nodded his head. 'I rather like that. Perhaps we could go further, and involve Western TV somehow. What do you think, David?'

'It would certainly take the initiative from them,' replied David after a pause. 'My only reservation is that if we do it *too* publicly, we'll risk giving them a credibility that they don't have at the moment.'

Don looked up. 'I think the fact that they've been on the telly has already given them all the credibility they need, David.'

'I take your point, Don. I still think our response should be low-key, though.'

'Well, either we do it, or we don't,' Sir said testily. 'I don't see how you can make it low-key. Or is it the involvement of television that bothers you?' he asked, daring David to criticize his idea.

David hesitated. 'I'm not sure. It needs thinking about. Television can be a double-edged sword,' he added with a smile.

'I think that rather depends on how it's handled,' said Sir, unwilling to concede the point. David didn't reply and he continued, 'Let's go round the table. What do you think, Michael?'

'I rather like the idea of inviting WANT to send us a representative. It puts *them* on the spot rather than us, and as Don said, they could no longer accuse us of hiding anything.'

Sir's face creased with irritation and I wondered what I'd said wrong, then I realized that David, next to me, had lit a cigarette.

'David, I do wish you wouldn't. You know how I feel about smoking, both personally and from the point of view of our company image.'

David stared back at him and for a moment I thought he was going to argue. Then he said,

'I'm sorry, Mr Harper. I forgot.'

He took a drag before stubbing it out in the glass ashtray in front of him, earning himself another poison look.

'Rhiannon?' Sir said at last.

She lifted her head, with its cap of short, dark red hair, from where she'd been doodling on the pad in front of her.

'I agree with Michael,' she said. Like David, she's Welsh, but with a prettier accent. 'Except in one respect. We've talked about putting WANT on the spot, and about taking the initiative from them. Perhaps we should try a more conciliatory approach. I suggest that we make a sincere effort to put our case across to their representative, and not treat her like an enemy.'

'Ah, the woman's point of view,' said Sir, smiling at her —rather patronizingly, I thought.

Between us, David still seethed.

'I think it's probably a bit late for that,' said Don. 'Liam Holford's death will have probably hardened their attitude.' He shrugged. 'We can but try, though.'

'John,' said Sir. 'What do you think?'

John Burton had been itching to say something, anything.

'I think there's another problem we may have overlooked.' John was our new whizzkid, young man on the make, and looked for all the world like the would-be gigolo in a certain well-known coffee advert on TV. 'There are certain areas into which we simply cannot allow *anyone* access—Radiation Areas like the Hot Cells, for instance. I think WANT could use that to our disadvantage, as well as twisting some of the things that they *do* see.'

'Don't you think that television coverage might help us there?' Sir asked gently.

'Er—perhaps it might,' replied John, who obviously didn't, but was equally unwilling to cross swords with Sir.

'Peter? What do you think?'

Peter raised his head like a tortoise coming out of its shell and spoke slowly and deliberately.

'After the television broadcast last night, we have no choice. We must invite WANT inside, publicly, and on a go-where-you-please basis. Only that way can we refute the accusation that we have something to hide.'

Peter always spoke slowly and deliberately, but from him, this was a speech of the highest eloquence, and it suddenly occurred to me that it sounded almost . . . rehearsed.

'If you don't mind my saying so, John,' Don said, 'I think your view might owe something to your inexperience. As Mr Harper said just now, it all depends on how it's handled. If we put our case properly, the public will understand perfectly well that there are certain areas in a Nuclear Power Station that have to be restricted. The most important thing is, that that case *must—be—put.*'

John's face tightened, but before he could reply, Sir nodded emphatically and said, 'And I think I'm right in saying that that appears to be the consensus of this meeting . . . yes, David?'

David drew in a breath. 'If we are to follow this course, I do suggest, most strongly, that we first make absolutely certain that there's nothing WANT can find to use against us.' He was trying to give way without losing too much face.

'I would have said that that was fairly obvious,' said Sir, denying him this. 'And also, fairly obviously, your responsibility.'

'Naturally,' David agreed. 'What I'm suggesting is that we give ourselves at least a week to make sure.'

'A week's too long. Today's Thursday. I suggest next Monday, Tuesday at the latest.' He paused. 'Which only leaves us to decide which of us is to escort her.'

'I suggest it has to be Don,' said Peter.

This was too much. I said, 'With all due respect to Don's well-known Irish charm and blarney, I would suggest

Rhiannon. If it *is* televised, it would look a lot better that way from our point of view. Woman to woman.'

Don said quickly, 'With all due respect to Rhiannon's well-known *Welsh* charm, she hasn't had quite my breadth of experience, and that might be important if any awkward questions come up. Although it's your decision, Mr Harper.' He smiled as he spoke, but I had the feeling he'd have willingly cut my throat if he could.

Sir pursed his lips in thought for a moment, then said, 'Attractive though the idea is—like Rhiannon herself—' he threw in, 'I think I go for Don's experience.' He looked around. 'I suggest we make this offer today, but for Monday or Tuesday, after David's satisfied himself that there's nothing they could find to use against us.'

The meeting had gone on for another hour after that without any more controversy, without any more useful ideas either. But another point had been made once again —that Sir didn't care very much for David.

Just after twelve, David stalked into my office.

'That bastard!' he said.

'Well, you did rather ask for it, lighting up in front of him. You know it's his pet hate.'

'I swear to God I forgot,' he said, taking out his cigarette packet now. 'I was trying to think at the time, and there was a sodding ashtray on the table. I just can't do a thing right for him.'

'No, you can't at the moment,' I agreed. 'And he was certainly out of line talking to you like that in front of the rest of us.'

'So what the hell can I do?'

'Not a lot, really.' I thought for a moment. 'If you're honestly asking me, I think you should keep your head down for a while. Just get on with your job as best you can and—'

'Keep my head down? Why the fuck should I? Am I or

am I not the Production Manager of this station? How would you like it if one of your blokes told you to keep your head down when I was around?'

'I wouldn't,' I agreed. 'But in your position, I'd probably do it.'

'Aaach!' He stubbed his fag in a shower of sparks. 'And as for his poxy ideas! I ask you! Kowtow to those bloody women in public and hand them credibility on a plate.'

'D'you really think it would do that?' I asked, curious.

'No,' he said, suddenly calm again, 'not really. It's a high risk strategy, though, and needs thinking through a lot more than either Sir or Don have done. For all his immaturity, John had a point. And Don is so glib he'll slip up on himself one day.'

'He's worse than glib, David. He's doing you real harm.'

He smiled, not very convincingly. 'He's trying to get the message across to Sir that Sir's predecessor gave my job to the wrong person. But real harm? No, I don't think so.'

'He is, and you're going to have to tread on him before too—'

'You haven't forgotten that you and Rhiannon are coming to dinner tomorrow evening, have you?'

I sighed. 'No David, I haven't forgotten.'

He looked at his watch. 'Fancy an early lunch?'

'No, thanks. Got things to do.'

'Suit yourself.'

I almost changed my mind then, but the truth was, I'd decided on a little high risk strategy myself.

CHAPTER 3

Jane was still there when I drove out, still standing with her placard. I didn't look at her directly, just saw her at the corner of my vision as I took a roundabout way to her village.

They lived in an end of terrace council house that they were in the process of buying. Steve answered the door after the second ring.

'Wha'do *you* want?'

'To say how sorry I am, Steve. To ask if there's anything I can do.'

His lips moved and I thought he was going to tell me to bugger off, then: 'You'd better come in. It's a mess, but tough.'

It was a mess, but he was worse. His fair hair was greasy, his face pale and unshaven. He smelt of sweat, whisky and cigarettes. He sat down and lit one now with trembling fingers. He'd given it up after Liam had gone into remission.

'You seen Jane?' he asked.

'Yes. I didn't know until then.'

He looked away. 'She hasn't cried, y'know. Not once since he died.'

'Have you?'

He took a long drag before replying. 'Yeah. Surprised me, that. Never thought I'd cry again.'

'Probably did you good.'

'Yeah. Maybe. Want a coffee or anything?'

'No, thanks.'

There was a short silence, then he said, 'You're a good bloke, Michael, but you can't come here any more. We're on opposite sides now.'

'Why do there have to be sides?'

'Liam died because of what you're doing. What *I* was once doing.'

'D'you really believe that?'

'I know it. There's proof. This professor down in South-ampton has proved it. Nuclear Power Stations have got to be closed down before they kill any more kids.' He spoke jerkily, like a faulty tape-recorder.

'Steve—' I touched my lips with the tip of my tongue— 'you've got to try and look forward, not back.'

'Forward? What the fuck've we got to look forward to? We can't even have any more kids.'

Dangerous ground. 'Why not, Steve?' I asked after a few seconds.

'More kids? More like Liam? How can we have more kids?'

'Even if that were true, which I don't believe it is, you'll have been away from the station for long enough by now—'

'That doctor, the one up in Sellafield. Said if you worked there, you should'n have kids. Didn' he? Eh?'

'He had his balls kicked in for saying that—'

'For telling the truth, perhaps.' He let out a long, shud-dering sigh. 'I dunno, Michael. But Jane says she won't have any more kids again. Not ever.'

'Give her a year and she'll—'

The door flung open and Jane came in. 'What're *you* doing here?' Low, choking voice—she'd seen my car out-side. I stood up. Two of the Women followed her in.

'I came to tell you—'

But she'd come forward and slapped my face. 'Get out of here. Get *out!*' she screamed, then collapsed sobbing on to the sofa.

One of the Women said to me, 'You'd better go. You've done enough damage.'

Steve was on the sofa with Jane. I went.

As I drove away, trembling myself now, the ironic

thought struck me that by making her cry, I might just have done Jane some good.

It wasn't until I got back to the station and saw that she wasn't in her usual place that I realized that one of the other Women with Jane had been the Gorgeous One.

I'd better explain about the Gorgeous One.

I noticed her the first day WANT picketed the station, said to myself, my God, she's gorgeous, and from that moment, the name had stuck in my mind. I suppose she was my Ideal Woman.

I looked out for her every day, when I arrived and when I left. She'd noticed me staring and once or twice she'd smiled, although usually she just gazed back neutrally. She was aware of me, though.

Maybe this makes me sound a bit odd, but I don't think I am particularly. I just needed a woman to think about.

Late the next morning, I had to go and see David about something. Don was with him in his office, but left as soon as I arrived.

'What did *he* want?' I asked.

'Oh, only to know whether I'd fixed up the date for having one of those women round.' He tried to speak lightly, but he was angry.

'And have you?'

'Probably next Tuesday.' He forced a smile. 'Sir had me along to his office earlier this morning, wanting to know what I'd done about it.'

'Oh?' I said.

'He was quite pleasant, actually. Offered me a glass of that vile sherry, which I felt obliged to accept. Asked me whether I was happy here, did my family miss Wales.' He snorted. 'I ask you—what does he think we are? Heathens with different customs?'

'Perhaps it was just his way of saying sorry for yesterday,'
I said.

'Hmm. He worries me when he's nice. I can't help thinking he must have something really nasty up his sleeve. Oh
well.' He paused. 'You haven't forgotten about tonight?'

'No, David,' I said.

'Will you be bringing Rhiannon?'

'Not much point really, considering she lives on the other
side of your place from me.'

'I suppose not.' He looked up. 'She's very fond of you,
you know.'

'I know. Don't try and matchmake, David. It doesn't
suit you.'

'Would you like some more, Rhiannon?' asked Helen
Rossily, knife poised over the steamed pudding.

I liked Helen. She had a rounded sexy body, pretty face
and warm voice, and I wondered again why David's eyes
and loins had such a wanderlust . . .

'I couldn't, thanks, Helen,' Rhiannon said. 'It was lovely,
but I haven't any more room.'

'I'd like some more, Mummy,' said Mark, their seven-
year-old son.

'You'd like some more—what?' demanded Megan, their
daughter.

'Some more—please,' said Mark sullenly. Megan, at
a year older, obviously felt responsible for her brother's
manners.

'Guests first,' said Helen. 'Would you like some more,
Michael?'

Mark gazed longingly at the pudding—there was just
enough left for two helpings—then hopefully up at me.

'No, thanks,' I said. 'It was lovely, though.'

'Megan?'

'I think I should have all of it, because Mark didn't say
please.'

'You shall have half each.'

As they tucked in, Helen went to fetch the coffee.

David turned to me and said, 'Do you do much work for the West Somerset Railway these days, Michael?' A constraint had hovered over the meal and he was making conversation.

'Not so much now.' I grinned at him. 'Pressure of work, y'know.'

'Ah.'

Mark looked up from his pudding. 'Daddy said if I asked you nicely, you might be able to take me for a ride on a steam engine.'

'Mark!' said Helen, coming back in.

'I didn't put it quite like that,' said David defensively.

'I should hope not.'

'It's all right,' I said, smiling. I turned to Mark. 'I'll see what I can do, although there's no promises. Footplate passes aren't the easiest things to get.'

'Thank you very much,' Mark said. 'And I'm sorry if I was rude.'

'That's all right.'

'If Michael can't get you one,' Rhiannon said to him, 'I'll fix you one for my diesel.'

'Thank you, Rhiannon.' He tried to sound enthusiastic, but diesel locomotives don't have quite the same attraction for small boys.

'How's your diesel coming along?' I asked her.

'Pretty well. Why don't you come along one evening next week and give me a hand?' She smiled at me. 'Pressure of work notwithstanding.'

'Yes, I'll do that.'

'Michael?' Mark looked up at me. 'Would you like to see my train set?'

'Not now, Mark,' said David. 'It's nearly your bedtime.'

'I don't mind,' I said. 'Just for a few minutes.'

'Be it on your own head.'

Mark's train set, quite a sophisticated one for a seven-year-old, was on a large table in an all-purpose room across the hall. A desk stood on one side with an old leather satchel on it, while on the other side were stacked boxes and suitcases.

'Oh, drat!' said Mark.

'What's the matter?' I asked, amused. Mark was shaping up like his father.

'I can't find the key. The key I start it with.' He pointed to a box with a keyhole beside the transformer. David had fitted up a small key-switch, presumably so that Mark wouldn't have to touch the mains. 'It was here yesterday.'

'Well, it can't have gone far. Let's have a look for it.'

'All right.' He dived under the table, so I looked along the stacked cases, and then under the desk.

No key.

As I lifted the satchel to look underneath, the flap fell open. Inside was a thick wad of WANT leaflets. As I closed the flap, Mark shouted, 'I've found it!' He got to his feet and triumphantly pushed it in, and a few seconds later a small goods train started whirring round the track.

Who on earth in this house would want WANT leaflets? I wondered.

David, perhaps?—Know thine enemy?

The door opened and Helen came in.

'Bed in five minutes, Mark, and no arguments.'

'All right, Mum,' he said resignedly.

She casually picked up the satchel and went out.

Liam's funeral was on Monday.

CHAPTER 4

Tuesday, and the Gorgeous One was in her usual position beside the gate as I drew up and showed my pass to the security guard. She showed no sign of recognition.

I glanced quickly behind as I drove away. She seemed to be staring after me, but she might have been looking at something else. The rest of the Women were blurred by the thick wire mesh surrounding the perimeter, their shapes and colours softened, like an Impressionist painting.

Perhaps it was my imagination again, but the whole station seemed slightly surreal that morning. It had rained during the night and we were back with the warm, hazy weather of late summer; even the Reactor Building seemed to take up and blend with the colour of the soft blue sky.

I checked that the gang knew what they were doing, made a few phone calls, then went through the draft of a report one more time before taking it along to the typing pool. My phone rang just as I was going out.

'Michael? It's David. I need to see you.'

'Two minutes?'

'OK, so long as it *is* two minutes.'

I explained what I wanted to the typist, then went along to his office. He was on the telephone himself when I walked in. He waved me to a chair.

David always put all of himself into whatever he happened to be doing at the time and now, his face and hands were moving as though he was actually tête-à-tête with the person on the other end of the phone . . .

'. . . you know I agree with you, Colin, it's just that things being the way they are . . .'

He was paler than usual this morning, and his voice sounded hoarse. His desk was the usual mess, overflowing

ashtray and papers held down with his very own paperweight, a mangled piston and connecting rod from some
long-deceased engine, now polished to a high shine.

I looked away, out of the window and over the perimeter
fence to the sea. The tide was in, cosily covering all the
rocks and mud and making the inflow rig, half a mile away,
look rather isolated, as though it were an oil rig. The dinghy
was tied against it; somebody must be playing with the new
underwater scanning equipment for which we were being
used as a test bed . . .

'. . . I'll be in touch then, Colin. 'Bye.' David put the
phone down and turned to me.

'Don hasn't turned up this morning, which leaves me
with a problem—you don't know where he is, do you?'

'Sorry, I don't. Hasn't he phoned in?'

'No, which, as I was saying, has left me with a problem.
If you remember, he was going to show one of the gang
outside over the station today—'

'Oh no, David, not me. I've got more than enough problems of my own—'

'I'm sure you have, but this is important, and—'

'Why don't you get Rhiannon to do it, like I suggested
at the meeting?'

'She's got today off. And John really *is* too busy.'

'What about Peter . . . ?' I suggested lamely . . .

'Oh, come on, Michael, I said this was important. Peter
has the charisma of a dead haddock.'

He had a point there, I had to admit.

'So you see,' David said, 'it has to be you. Sorry.'

I knew when I was beaten. 'When?'

He looked up at his clock. 'Ten-thirty. Which gives you
about twenty minutes.'

'Thanks,' I said drily. 'How much detail do I go into?'

'As much as you like, within reason.' He hesitated. 'The
thing is, we know she's probably just hoping to spot some

dirt, so keep it smooth and simple and don't lose your temper.'

That was rich, coming from him. 'What's her name?'

He looked down at the paper on his desk. 'Ms Sarah Brierly. She'll be in Reception. Oh, and Doc Fitzpatrick asked especially if he could see her at some stage.'

I went along to the rest-room and fortified myself with black coffee while I thought about what I was going to say. It was easier in one respect—WANT themselves had asked that the tour be low-key, probably realizing that the double-edged-sword aspect of television could work both ways.

One last coffee, then the Gents' to check my appearance (inoffensive brown eyes, straight nose, reasonably good-humoured mouth, etc . . .) before going down to reception to meet Ms Brierly. Who, of course, was the Gorgeous One.

'Ms Brierly? Michael Hempstead. I've been asked to show you round the station.'

She stood up. 'Hello.' Firm handshake for a woman, cool and assured, like her cultured voice. 'Forgive me, but I was told it was to be a Mr Waterford.'

'So it was, but I'm afraid he's now unavailable. You'll have to make do with me.'

I wanted to kick myself for saying that, but she made no reaction, just said, 'Shall we go, then?'

Suddenly, embarrassed by my own awkwardness, I wanted to do a good job.

'Before we do, it would help me to know how much you already know, and what you'd like to see.'

'Very well.'

'Shall we sit down?'

'If you like.'

We sat.

It's strange how a familiar face looks when you get close to it for the first time. It was the face I looked for every morning: oval, with high forehead and long brown hair worn up, but firmed out now by the light from behind us. The fine-grained skin, proud mouth, the fineness of her hair, the candour in her large grey eyes . . . She was waiting for me to say something . . .

'Er—have you visited a power station before—any type of power station?'

'No.'

'Well, in principle, they're all the same. You boil water to make steam to drive an electric generator. Some boil the water by burning coal or oil, we do it with a nuclear reaction, that's the only difference.'

'Can I stop you there, Mr Hempstead? Obviously, I'm against nuclear power, but I don't want to argue about that now, I'm here to listen and learn. You asked me whether there was anything I particularly wanted to see. The answer is yes, the nuclear reactors themselves, the facilities for storage and transport of spent fuel and the inlet and outlet systems for the sea-water coolant. Perhaps we could do that?'

By way of answer, I leaned back in my chair and smiled a forced smile.

'I didn't mean to patronize you, you obviously know more than I was led to believe. Shall we start again?'

She stiffened slightly, then relaxed and smiled herself, a real one.

'Yes, all right.'

'You'd like to see the Reactor Hall, the way we handle spent fuel and the sea-water cooling system?'

'Yes.'

I stood up. 'Then let's start with the reactors, shall we?'

'Fine.' She held up a camera. 'I was told it would be all right if I took some photographs.'

'Sure.'

She rose easily and passed through the darkened glass door I held open for her. I followed her into the sunshine.

She would have been about six years younger than me,

I thought, say twenty-five, and six inches shorter, say five feet five. Her body moved fluently beneath the calf-length cotton dress, a well-shaped body, not too slender. Her legs were bare.

She turned to me. 'So the job of showing me round was rather dropped on you?'

'Yes. Half an hour ago.'

'It's not something you normally do?'

'No. Don Waterford usually does it. He's part Irish and has the blarney.'

'I see.' We walked a few more paces. 'The humming that's always in the background, that would be the generators?'

'The turbines. Which is where we're going, so I'd better give you these now.'

She stopped. 'Give me what?'

'Ear plugs.' I handed her a plastic pack. 'It's very noisy in the Turbine Hall, that's where the turbines and generators are. We have to go through it to get to the reactors.'

'D'you want me to put them in now?'

'We might as well, since we're nearly there.'

I showed her how to fit them and a moment later opened the door to the Turbine Hall. She made a face as the noise enveloped us.

I led her past the massive, brightly painted generators and turbines to the steps up to the lift. I motioned for her to go first. About half way up she stopped to look at the vast, apparently tangled mass of stainless steel pipework that served the turbines. Then, shaking her head slightly, she moved on.

In the lift the noise faded.

'Can I take these out now?' she shouted, then grinned. 'Sorry. You were right about the noise.' Then, 'How can anyone possibly understand all that plumbing?'

I shrugged. 'You get used to it.'

The lift stopped and I opened the door into the lobby of the Reactor Hall.

''Morning, Michael,' said the little man behind the desk.

'Hello, Ernie. This is Ms Brierly. I'm showing her over the reactor.'

'You'll be wantin' a couple of film badges, then. There you go, miss,' he said, handing one to her. Female emancipation hasn't caught up with Ernie yet.

'What do I do with it?' she asked me.

'Pin it on somewhere you can see it. The panel here—' I showed her—'turns black if you're exposed to any radiation.'

'Oh,' she said. 'I take it that's not very likely?'

I looked at Ernie, who said, 'Never known one to go in fifteen years, miss.'

I thanked him, then escorted her along the corridor and held open the door at the end.

'Oh,' she said again as we emerged. I wasn't surprised. The first view of the inside of the Reactor Hall takes most people that way.

It's about a hundred by two hundred feet, and a hundred feet high. We were about seventy feet up and the people working at ground level looked like clockwork figures that had just been wound up.

'Where is the reactor?' she asked.

'We're standing on it.'

'Oh,' she said for the third time. She looked down at her badge. 'How long do these take to work?'

'Pretty well instantaneously.'

'It's so quiet. I can't even hear the turbines now.'

'No.'

'For some reason I expected it to be noisy.'

'Most people do.'

She drew in a breath, then raised her camera and took several shots before bringing out a notebook. 'Well, you'd better tell me how it works.'

'It's a British Advanced Gas Reactor, or AGR.' I pointed along the top of the pile. 'Each of those squares you can see covers a nuclear core. Each core consists of rods of uranium fuel which have been bombarded with neutrons to start the nuclear reaction. Once it's started, the reaction releases further neutrons which keeps it going. We then control it by raising or lowering boron rods into the cores which absorb the neutrons. Follow me so far?'

'I think so. But tell me,' she went on quickly, 'why aren't our badges turning black?'

I grinned. 'Because the reactor's surrounded by twenty feet of reinforced concrete.'

'And the radiation can't get through that?'

'No.'

'Not even gamma radiation?'

'Not even gamma radiation.'

She looked down at her badge again. 'I suppose I'll have to take your word for that. Boron rods, you were saying.'

'Yes. So we've got a controlled nuclear reaction which gives off heat, a lot of heat. That heat is taken up by a gas, carbon dioxide in this reactor, which is circulating round the fuel rods. The gas transfers the heat to water, which turns to steam and drives the turbines.'

She was frowning in concentration as she scribbled. 'Are each of these systems closed? I mean,' she continued, 'does the gas become radioactive? And if so, does the water?'

'Yes, they are closed systems. The gas does become radio-active, to an extent, but the water doesn't.'

'What happens when there's a leak between the systems?'

'In that extremely unlikely event, the boron control rods automatically drop back into the cores and the system shuts down.'

Her eyes turned to me. 'But that didn't happen at Chernobyl, did it?'

'The Leningrad type reactor, the one at Chernobyl, is of

a design that was rejected by this country back in the 'fifties as being fundamentally flawed.'

She smiled. 'That's very easy for you to say, but I'm afraid it doesn't persuade me. Or a lot of other people.'

I took a breath. 'I told you just now about the closed systems, reactor to gas, gas to water, right?'

She didn't say anything.

'In the Leningrad reactor, there's no gas step. The uranium heats the water directly, which turns into radioactive steam and drives the turbines before going back to the reactor. Nothing like so secure a system.'

Still she smiled. 'You're preaching to the unconvertible.'

I smiled back. 'So I can see.'

'So why don't you tell me how you take out the spent fuel? That's highly radioactive, isn't it? D'you do it while the reactor's still working?'

'We could, but we don't.'

I explained how we shut the reactor down and sheathed the spent fuel cores in boron before winching them out.

'And then they're put on the train to Sellafield?' she said innocently.

I laughed. 'That's misleading and inaccurate, as I'm sure you know very well.'

'So what does happen?'

'The spent fuel's stored in cooling ponds for three months until the worst of the radiation has died down, then it's packed into stainless steel flasks, and then a purpose built train takes it to Sellafield for processing.'

'Into nuclear weapons grade plutonium.'

'No,' I said firmly, 'it is not.' It's a misconception that always irritates me. 'Ninety-seven per cent of the spent fuel from here is reprocessed into re-usable fuel—it's something that this country is still very good at.'

'Yes, but what happens to the other three per cent?'

'It's treated and stored.'

'Where?'

'Underground at Sellafield.'

'For how long?'

'Er—indefinitely,' I said, aware of the trap I'd walked into.

'Thank you. You've just defined for me why I shall always be against nuclear power. You're deliberately creating very dangerous substances that can't then be uncreated. You just store them somewhere and hope for the best. What kind of legacy is that to leave for future generations?'

'It's a question of degree. In thirty years of nuclear power generation, this country has produced enough high level waste to fill a pair of semi-detached houses. Surely it isn't beyond the wit of man to contain those kinds of quantities safely.'

'The wit of man,' she mused. 'Yes. It's always the men who insist on going boldly where none have gone before, and the women who have to pick up the pieces. Or try to warn.'

'Perhaps I should have said humankind.'

'But you didn't, did you?' She grinned, pleased with herself. 'Come on, back to the grind. Can I see the storage ponds now, please?'

I looked at my watch. 'There's a job going on there at the moment, so I suggest we look at the sea-water cooling system first.' Her cockiness had piqued me slightly.

'All right.'

She didn't speak again until we were outside, when she said, 'Why d'you need sea-water? What does it cool?'

'You know the huge towers you see at coal-fired power stations?'

She nodded.

'The sea-water does the same job they do, which is to condense the steam back into water after it's been through the turbines.'

'Why d'you need to do that? Isn't it a waste of energy?'

'Not at all. You need a drop in pressure on the exhaust

side of the turbine, a vacuum, if you like, to pull the steam through and get the most out of its energy. Then the condensed water can be pumped back into the boiler.'

She thought about this, then nodded slowly.

We came to the seaward side of the station where we could see over the perimeter fence.

'You see that rig out there? That's where the water's taken in.'

'Why is it so far out?'

'There's a terrific rise and fall of tide here, up to forty feet. A spring tide can go out to within a hundred feet of that rig.'

'All right, so the water's taken in, then what happens?'

'It's filtered to remove debris. You see those things over there that look a bit like millwheels? They're drum screens that catch all the junk that comes in with the water.'

'Can I see?'

'Sure.'

We walked over. Being high tide, the Drum Screen Pits were nearly full. The drum screens slowly revolved, to emerge dripping from the opaque water and deposit their cargo of weed and jetsam into the skips.

'Ugh!' Sarah said suddenly. 'Is that an eel? It's still alive!'

'We get quite a few of them. We feed them to the gulls.' I looked at my watch again. 'Shall we go and—'

'What's that?' she said sharply, gripping my arm. 'Michael, there's something in the water . . .'

'Where? I can't see any . . .'

But then I did. A whiteness glimmering just beneath the surface of the cloudy water, rolling in the current . . . then a face emerged, eyes peering sightlessly—

Even swollen in death, even with the crabs clinging to his nose like an obscene moustache, I could recognize the coarsely handsome face of Don Waterford.

CHAPTER 5

With a cry, she buried her face in my shoulder, her fingers digging into my arms.

'It's all right,' I said, my hands round her shoulders.

'It's not all right.' Her voice was muffled. 'It's horrible.'

'Yes.'

A wolf-whistle jerked my head up—one of the cooling plant workers. I gave him a wave to keep him away, then said, 'We'd better go over to Reception and raise the alarm.'

'Yes.'

She'd regained control of herself and we walked, slowly at first, then more quickly to the darkened glass doors.

'Sharon,' I said to the receptionist when we were inside, 'there's been an accident and Ms Brierly has had a shock. Could you get her some coffee, please, while I—'

'A glass of water will be fine, thank you,' Sarah said from where she was sitting.

'It's no trouble—' began Sharon.

'Really. Just a glass of water.'

As soon as Sharon had gone, I keyed in David's number.

'Rossily,' he said curtly.

'It's Michael. I've found Don. He's dead, in the Drum Screen Pits.'

'Bloody hell.' Then, 'Are you sure?'

'Yes. Do you want to ring the police, or shall I?'

'You do it. You'd better have the flow in that pit shut off as well. Michael, does anyone else know . . . ?'

'Yes. If you remember . . .'

'Oh my God,' he said tiredly. 'Ms Brierly.'

'That's right.'

'Listen, Michael, make sure she stays there until the police arrive, don't let her anywhere near a phone—'

'All right, I'll do what I can.' I broke the connection and rang the police at Newbridge, who said they'd have someone there directly. Then I got through to the Control Room and told them to shut the relevant pump off. As I put the phone down, I noticed that Sharon had come back with the water for Sarah.

I went over to her. 'Feeling any better?'

'A bit.' She drank some of the water. 'What happens now?'

'The police'll be here soon and—'

'Shouldn't one of us have stayed there?' she interrupted. 'By the body?'

'Perhaps. But I had to phone my boss, and I didn't think you'd have wanted to stay there.'

'No.' She drank more water. 'I suppose I'll have to stay until they get here.'

'Yes. They'll want statements from both of us.'

She looked at her watch. 'I hope they'll be here before too long . . . Is there a phone I could use?'

I hesitated. 'Probably better if you didn't just now.'

'Better for whom?' she flashed.

'The police won't be long.'

Nor were they. We heard the siren a few minutes later as she took the glass back to Sharon and thanked her.

David had heard the siren too and came in just before they did. There were four of them, the most senior being a tall, stone-faced Chief Inspector rather inappropriately called Doll. One of them, a sergeant, stayed to take a statement from Sarah while David and I took the others to the Drum Screen Pits.

As soon as we were out of the door, David told Doll who Sarah was. 'It would be a great help, Chief Inspector, if she could be asked—instructed—not to contact the Press for the moment.'

'You will all be very strongly advised not to contact the Press,' Doll replied. 'Failure to follow that advice would

render you liable to prosecution for obstructing the police.'
Which is what David wanted to hear, although perhaps not
quite in that way.

The body was as I'd left it, floating just below the surface
of the now still water. David told Doll how the pit worked,
then Doll sent one of the others for some equipment from
their car.

We both had to stay while the body was recovered in
order to make a formal identification, then we went back
to reception with Doll.

Sarah had already left. Doll told the sergeant who'd taken
her statement to go to Don's house and break the news to
his wife, and one of the others to cordon off the area around
the Drum Screen Pits. The rest of us went to David's office,
where I made a brief statement describing how I'd found
the body, then Doll questioned us both together while his
constable took notes.

Had Don been at work yesterday? Yes, we answered.

Had he been upset, or worried about anything?

'No,' I said. 'If anything, he seemed to be happier than
usual.'

'I noticed that too,' David said.

'Any idea why?'

We shook our heads.

Was he normally a happy man? Yes.

No recent problems, either at home or work? No, not
that we knew of.

So suicide wasn't likely? Unlikely, we thought.

Accident? Possible, we supposed, although Don had
worked at the station for many years.

Doll glanced at the constable who was busily scribbling
this all down before continuing.

'So we may have to consider foul play. I'm sure you both
noticed the marks on his forehead.'

'Couldn't they have been caused by the drum screens?' I
asked.

'That'll be for the pathologist to say. Anyway, you can appreciate how important it is that we find out who saw him last. How about you, Mr Hempstead?'

'I last saw him late in the afternoon, a little after four.'

'Where would that have been?'

'In the rest-room, drinking coffee.'

'And you didn't see him any later than that?'

'No.'

'Not even as he left?'

'No.'

'How about you, Mr Rossily?'

'I did see him later, at about five. He came here to my office to discuss something.'

'What would that have been, sir?'

'The arrangements for showing Ms Brierly around the station. It was to have been his job.'

'For how long was he here?'

'About fifteen minutes, I'm not sure exactly.'

'And after that?'

'I assumed he'd gone home.'

'Did you actually see him leave?'

'No, I didn't.'

'Is there any way we can check? You seem to have pretty tight security here.'

'I can do that now if you like.'

Doll liked, so David rang security at the main gate, who told him that Don had left the station at five thirty-five, but returned at seven-thirty.

'Interesting. Is that usual, sir?'

'Not unusual, in this job. I was here myself until a little after eight.'

'I see, sir. Didn't you see him then?'

'No, I didn't. I was with the Station Manager, Mr Harper, in his office, and—'

The phone rang. David picked it up, grunted and held it out to Doll. 'For you, Chief Inspector.'

Doll said 'Yes' and 'I see' a few times before replacing it.

'That was Sergeant Hadleigh,' he said. 'Apparently Mrs Waterford and her children are visiting her mother in London, so I'll have to arrange for someone up there to break the news to her.'

He paused on this sombre note, then said to David, 'Do you know why Mr Waterford would have come back here when he did, sir?'

'No idea, unless it was something to do with this visit. Have you any idea, Michael?'

'No, but Peter might.'

'That's a point . . .'

'Who is Peter, sir?'

'Peter Broomfield,' said David. 'He's—he was Don's closest friend here. They were both Charge Engineers, Don in the Reactor Hall, Peter at the Cooling Ponds.'

'Is he here today?' asked Doll.

'Yes,' I said. 'I saw him early this morning.'

'I'll speak to him next,' said Doll, making a note in his book. 'Is there an office I could use? I'll be needing to speak to all Mr Waterford's colleagues.'

'I suppose you could use Don's,' said David, after a pause. 'If that doesn't seem too morbid.'

'No, sir. We'll be needing to make an examination of it, anyway. One more thing,' he continued, 'since we may have to consider foul play, I must ask you whether Mr Waterford had any enemies.'

David made a mouth. 'Some people liked him, some didn't. I wouldn't have thought he had any enemies, as such.'

'Did you like him?'

'Not particularly, no.'

'Why was that, sir?'

'For the oldest reason in the world, Chief Inspector. He thought he could do my job better than me.'

'I see. And this caused you problems?'

'Problems, yes, but not insurmountable ones.'

Doll regarded him a moment before turning to me. 'How about you, Mr Hempstead?'

'I'm afraid I didn't like him much, either.'

'Oh. And why was that, sir?'

'He was cynical, hard. He liked to stir up trouble.'

'I see. Perhaps I should have asked you who *did* like him?'

We both smiled reluctantly.

'Well, there was Peter Broomfield, whom I've already mentioned,' said David. 'And Don's subordinates generally. He was always good to the men under him. He looked after them.'

'Would you agree with that, Mr Hempstead?'

'Yes. He could be kind, even generous to his subordinates. It was his peers and immediate superiors he had problems with.'

He turned back to David. 'What about his home life?'

'Good, so far as I know. But you'd better ask Peter Broomfield about that.'

'Ah yes, Mr Broomfield. Does he know yet, by the way?'

'I haven't told him, although he's probably seen your men and wondered what's happening.'

'I'd better speak to him now.' Doll hesitated. 'I think for the moment I'd prefer to treat this as an accidental death. So if I could ask you both not to say anything about our discussion for the moment . . .'

We both gave our assurances, then Doll said he'd finished with me for the moment, so I went back to my own office. I sat there for several minutes, absorbing the shock, then one of the shift engineers rang through with a problem which took up most of the rest of the day, which was perhaps just as well.

More police arrived, the forensic team I supposed, and started working round the Drum Screen Pits. Then the news obviously got round, because a sort of silence seemed to descend over the station, although the noise of the machinery stayed the same.

David found me a little before four and told me that most people had assumed Don's death to be an accident, although Peter had taken the news badly.

'It's still hard to believe, isn't it?' he said.

'Not for me. Not after I found him.'

'I don't mean the fact that he's dead, it's the foul play part of it.'

'It must have been an accident,' I said. 'Although I can't understand how it could have happened.'

'Let's hope so.'

Things were under control a bit before six, so I packed up to go home. On the way out I looked for Sarah, but she wasn't in her usual place and I had a sudden small desolate feeling that I wasn't going to see her again. Rather stupid really, considering that our meeting had hardly been a success.

I live in a village about five miles from the station in a small cottage that looks better than it is. Curious, I thought as I unlocked the door, the relationship between an old house and those who live in it. Each has to compromise, but the 'owner' usually rather more.

Church Acre Cottage had been a sullen and unkempt little brute when I'd bought it. It took me a year to render it kempt, but it had remained sullen until Julia arrived. I don't know how she did it, but it was as though the cottage had said to itself, 'Ah, this is more like it,' and smiled. It hadn't seemed so cold in the winter either, and in summer a pair of house martins had nested under the eaves, although perhaps they'd done it before and I just hadn't noticed.

Maybe you'll say it was all in the mind, but the fact is, the place smiled when she arrived and went back to being sullen when she left. Perhaps the little brute had understood

that once I'd got over the shock of her leaving, I found that
being on my own again quite suited me in some ways. No
more painful digs in the ribs for snoring, or being nagged
for coming home from work late.

Loneliness? I don't mind my own company and have
plenty to keep me occupied.

I got rid of my tie, pulled on some jeans and turned
on the radio for the news (no more compulsory television).

Dinner. Had an omelette yesterday, so not eggs. Fish,
perhaps . . .

Something on the radio caught my attention and I turned
it up . . .

> The Government has announced that it will review the
> future of Nuclear Power in this country once the Pressur-
> ized Water Reactor has been built at Sizewell. Com-
> pletion is due in 1994.

Another two years of uncertainty, I thought. What
with Sweden having announced that it was phasing out
Nuclear Power, and no new reactors built in America for
nearly twenty years, we were all getting a little twitchy
about our future at Somerset Nuclear Electric. Although I
didn't think that the Government would actually close
any nuclear stations before their lifespan was over . . .
Did I?'

I went to the freezer and found some cod.

> . . . the Opposition spokesman on Energy condemned
> the 'botched' privatization of the Power Industry, and
> the 'calamitous' proposals to privatize the Coal industry,
> which would necessitate the closure of a third of the
> mines. The building of gas-fired power stations, he said,
> the so-called 'dash-for-gas', would be to sacrifice one pre-
> cious asset on the altar of profit, while at the same time
> destroying another—coal.

He had a point. Gas reserves were said by some to be as little as fifteen years, and coal mines are an awful lot easier to shut than they are to re-open.

The Future of the Power Industry is Wide Open, the optimists were saying. And about as powerful as a bullock's prick, they were saying at Desolation Point.

I grilled the cod with a little oil. Sauté potatoes and a cheese sauce. Great! But for some reason a disquiet, a malaise fastened on to me after I'd finished the meal and washed up.

No washing or ironing needed to be done. No jobs on the house or garden outstanding. Not even anything worthwhile on the box.

I knew what it was. Although I was sorry about Don's death, I couldn't feel truly sad about it. Oh, I was sorry for his wife and kids, I just couldn't feel truly sorry for his absence . . .

On impulse, I pulled on a light jacket, went out of the back door of the cottage and up into the fields behind. From the top of the rise you can see the sea, just two miles away. The tide was nearly in again, sea mirror calm. I walked to the next village.

Thought about Don and told myself not to think ill of the dead. Wished it were dusk. I can lose myself in the dusk.

Foul play. Doll had made it sound like something in a game of football.

The pub in Stoke Robert, the Queen's Head, is better than the one in my own village, beams and stone floor, although if the landlord isn't careful with the horse brasses and other of ye olde artefacts, it's going to end up as ye olde caricature of itself.

I went in. A crowd of people were laughing boisterously in one corner. I didn't feel like talking to the landlord, so I took my beer over to the window, meaning to drink it fairly quickly and leave. I'd barely taken a mouthful when a voice behind me said, 'Hello. Mind if I join you?'

It was Sarah.

CHAPTER 6

I twisted round to look at her. 'No, of course I don't.' I pulled out a chair. Its legs scratched noisily on the stone floor. 'Can I get you a drink?'

'No, thanks, I've already got one over there,' she said as she sat down. 'I wanted to thank you for the trouble you went to this morning.'

'Oh, that's all right. I'm only sorry about . . . what happened. It can't have been very nice for you.'

'No. Have the police discovered yet how it happened?'

'No. Or at least, if they have, they haven't told us.'

'Are they still there? The police?'

'I think they've finished looking for forensic evidence now, although there are still some of us to be questioned.'

She said, 'It was an accident, wasn't it?'

'So far as I know,' I lied.

I wanted to ask what the police had said to her, whether they'd told her not to contact the Press, but couldn't think how to put it without seeming offensive . . .

She said suddenly, 'Look, I hope this doesn't seem callous, but I would very much like to see the rest of the station.'

'I'm sure that can be arranged.'

'Could you find out and let me know?'

'Sure.'

She hesitated. 'Is there any chance you could let me know tomorrow?'

'I can try. Is it that urgent?'

'Yes, it is. Really.'

I didn't say anything, and seeing that more was required,

she continued, 'I may have to go back home tomorrow evening, and it would be a great help to me if I could get this finished before then.'

'So you actually want to see the rest of the station tomorrow?'

'If possible, please.'

'As I said, I can try. Where will you be? In your usual place?'

She smiled faintly, knowingly. 'Yes—probably. If not, you can contact me here.'

'This is where you're staying?'

'Yes. When I'm not showing solidarity with the troops and camping.' She hesitated again for an instant, then went on quickly, 'It's very good of you to go to all this trouble —especially when I'm working against you.'

'Routine Company policy, ma'am,' I said. Then, 'If we weren't completely open with you, then it might look as though we really *did* have something to hide, mightn't it?'

'I . . . suppose it might.'

'So we emphasize the fact that we don't have anything to hide by being as open and helpful as we can.'

She smiled. 'OK, you've made your point.'

'So I'll see what I can do.'

'Thanks.'

I suppose I was expecting her to make a few more polite noises and go back to her friends, but she didn't. She said, 'D'you live near here? Is this your local pub?'

'No. I live in Woodford, the next village along.'

'Oh yes, I've been through it. So what brought you over here tonight?'

'Difficult to say,' I said, thinking of Don. Then it occurred to me that she might think I'd come over because of her, so I said, 'The man we found today, Don Waterford, I didn't always get on with him. This evening I couldn't stop thinking about him, so I walked over here to try and get it out of my system.'

'In other words, you were feeling guilty.'

'I think guilt's maybe too strong a word. Disquiet.'

'Was he married?'

'Yes. Two kids.'

'It's them I feel sorry for.' She said this with feeling.

'Yes.'

'Have they been told yet?'

'His wife probably has been by now, I don't know about the children. They were all away in London.'

'How old are they?'

'Around eight and ten, I think.'

She sighed. 'Not a good age for them.'

'No.'

'Well—' she pushed her chair back—'I mustn't keep you.'

'You weren't.'

Again, the faintly mocking smile. 'No. Well, I'll see you tomorrow, then.'

She went back to her friends and I quickly finished my drink and left.

It was dusk now, and something in my mind freed itself.

She knew how I felt about her, she'd as much as acknowledged it, and she was using it for her own ends—to an extent, anyway. That didn't bother me unduly, so long as I could stay in touch with her.

The walk purged me of something else as well. As soon as I got home, I sat down and wrote a letter to Don's wife, Shirley, and took it down to the postbox in the village.

The next morning she was in her usual place and gave me a smile and a wave as I drove in, which earned me a half envious, half curious look from the security guard who checked my pass. I was still smiling to myself as I parked and switched the engine off, then I looked up to see the near naked head, with its ring of grey hair, of Peter

Broomfield, sitting in his car next to me. He was staring into space, oblivious of me, of everything.

I got out, pulled the tonneau over and zipped it, then went over to him. He blinked and shook his head as he became aware of me, then opened his door and got out.

'Hello, Michael. Sorry—miles away.'

'That's all right. Peter, I'm so sorry about Don.'

He didn't answer for a moment, then said, 'Yes. Thanks. I still can't take it in.'

I looked at him closely. His eyes were bloodshot and had dark pouches under them. His normally pale skin was like paper. He'd always looked older than his forty-five years, especially since his divorce, but today he looked nearer sixty. He must have noticed me staring because he said, 'Couldn't sleep last night thinking about it. Couldn't sleep at all.'

I said, 'You should have taken the day off. Nobody would have minded.'

'Oh no,' he said seriously. 'Couldn't do that. Besides, the police want to see me.'

'Didn't they do that yesterday?'

'Yes. Said they wanted to see me again today.'

'But why?' Not the most tactful question perhaps, but I really couldn't see Peter being suspected of anything.

He shrugged. 'Maybe because I'm—I was—a friend of Don's. Maybe because they think I can . . . Oh, I don't know. Come on, let's go in.'

I walked over to the main block with him.

'Have you seen Shirley at all?' I asked.

'I spoke to her last night. On the phone.'

'How is she?'

'Pretty bad, as you'd expect. Pretty bad,' he said again.

'Is there anybody with her?'

'Her mother, who's usefulness is debatable. They're all coming back sometime today.'

'Go and see David after the cops have spoken to you,' I

urged. 'He'll understand if you want to take some of the load from Shirley.'

'Yeah,' he said. 'I might do that. Thanks, Michael.' He turned away to his office, not wanting to talk any more, and I was sure he wouldn't go to see David.

As I went up to my own office, I pondered on the relationship between the two men. It had seemed incongruous at first, because they'd been so different, but thinking about it, perhaps it had been synergistic. Perhaps a repressed person like Peter needed an extrovert like Don to dominate him . . . In which case, what was Peter going to do now?

I dumped my case, checked my work list for the day, then did the rounds to make sure everyone knew what they were doing. Then I went along to David's office to ask about Sarah's visit.

''Morning, Michael,' he said as I went in. 'We were just talking about you.'

Doll was with him.

'Oh?' I said.

'Would you like to sit down for a moment, Mr Hempstead?' said Doll. I glanced at David, but he didn't seem to mind this trespass on his territory, so I sat.

'I was just telling Mr Rossily,' continued Doll, 'that we've now had a preliminary PM report. It appears that Mr Waterford was killed by several blows to the head with a blunt instrument. In other words, murder.'

A picture of Don's bloated face as he'd been pulled out of the Drum Screen Pit flashed in front of me . . .

'The pathologist says he was killed sometime between six and ten o'clock, although we're hoping for a more accurate estimate than that. If we assume it was done by someone here at the power station, we're going to have to find them by elimination. Now, I believe you told me you last saw Mr Waterford in the afternoon, at about four.'

'That's right.'

'So let's move on to the evening. You would have left the station at about five?'

I glanced at David. 'A bit before that, about four-thirty. I had something to attend to.' In truth, it was nearer to four, but David could be a bit of a stickler for time-keeping. Be sure your sins will find you out.

'All right,' said Doll. 'What did you do then?'

'I drove to Newbridge, stayed there for about half an hour, then drove home.'

'What time did you arrive home?'

'About six.'

'And then?'

'I cooked a meal, ate it, washed up, wrote some letters, watched the news on TV, then read a little before going to bed.'

'Any witnesses to any of that?'

'The person I saw in Newbridge would remember, but otherwise no.'

'You live alone?'

'Yes.'

'All right. If you could go down to the office we're using and make a statement to that effect, please, that will be all for the moment.'

'I came to ask Mr Rossily something.' I turned to David. 'Ms Brierly has asked me if I could show her round the rest of the station today. Is that all right with you?'

'Today? You'd have thought she'd seen enough yesterday. However, so long as the Chief Inspector has no objections . . .' He looked at Doll, who shook his head.

'When did she ask you?' said David. 'If I remember, she'd cleared off by the time we got back from the Drum Screen Pits yesterday.'

'Yesterday evening, as a matter of fact,' I said, trying to sound casual. 'I went for a walk and happened to run into her at—'

David held up his hands. 'You don't have to make expla-

nations to me, Michael,' he said, grinning. 'Fast work,
though.'

To my fury, I felt myself flushing and went out before it
became obvious. I went straight down to Don's office and
made a statement to Sergeant Hadleigh, then went over to
the main gate to find Sarah.

'Just want a word with one of the ladies,' I explained to
the guard. He still made me log out, though.

'Hello,' said Sarah. 'Any luck?'

'Yes.' Now I was with her, my throat felt like closing up.

'Oh, well done.' She looked absolutely ravishing. Her
face had a healthy flush, her eyes sparkled and her hair,
loosely bound, was fresh and springy. She wore a mini-dress
and her legs were evenly tanned. Her scent made my head
swim. 'When can we start?'

I looked at my watch. 'It'll have to be after lunch, now.
Say one-thirty?'

'Oh.' Her face fell slightly, then quickly recovered into
a smile. 'That'll be fine. What will you do? Come over for
me?'

'If you like.'

'I like. I'll see you then.'

I became aware that all the Women nearby had been
staring at us, and as she turned back to them, one or two
of them whistled. She silenced them with a gesture.

And then the guard who logged me back in winked and
said, 'Thinking of changing sides, sir? Can't say that I
blame you.'

This is getting unfunny, I thought. Is she worth all this
embarrassment?

Yes.

CHAPTER 7

She said, 'Being here makes me feel a bit like a voyeur.'

We were in the soundproof gallery above the nerve centre of the station, the Control Room. There were half a dozen or so people below us working, checking the banks of VDUs, fine tuning some of the arrays of control knobs, or just chatting over coffee, all blissfully aware of us.

She turned back to me from the glass. 'I thought you told me that everything here was controlled by computer?'

'So it is, by and large.'

'So what are those people doing?'

'Making minor adjustments. Monitoring the temperatures, flow rates and so on. There are manual overrides on all the systems in case of emergency.'

'Doesn't that leave the system as a whole open to human error, as in Chernobyl or Three Mile Island?'

'No. Suppose some lunatic overrode the computer and allowed the nuclear reaction to accelerate to a potentially dangerous level. The boron control rods in the reactor would automatically drop back into the cores and stop the reaction, and the safety-valves on the boiler would blow. It's what we call a Scram.'

'Why Scram?'

'It was originally an American term that came about because they used to evacuate the building when it happened. We still call it a Scram, although we don't evacuate the building now. It happens in any potentially hazardous situation.'

'You've got an answer for everything, haven't you?'

'Not me, the system. And it has several answers for everything, so that in the unlikely event of one of them failing, there are several back-ups.'

'As I said, an answer for everything.'

We stayed a bit longer while she took photos, then she said, 'Perhaps you'd show the Cooling Pond pumps now.'

We'd been down to see the Cooling Ponds beneath the reactors earlier; now she wanted to see the pumps that circulated the pond water.

We went back outside and I led her round the other side of the Reactor Building to the Pump House. I found my card-key and inserted it into the slot, pulled open the door and switched on the light. The electric motors inside whined busily.

'Are those the pumps?' she asked.

'The motors. The pumps themselves are behind.' I pointed.

'And they circulate the pond water?'

'Yes.'

'Which is radioactive?'

'To an extent. Most of the radioactivity has precipitated out before it gets to the pump.'

'But it *is* radioactive?'

'As I said, to an extent.'

'I can't understand why this should be accessible from the outside. Isn't that a security hazard?'

'Not unless the lunatic I mentioned earlier, who also happened to have the right card-key, broke in and put a bomb on one of the pumps. It certainly would be a hazard if a pump broke down and couldn't be easily repaired because it was inaccessible.'

'Hmm.' She adjusted the flash on her camera and took a few shots.

'Is there anything else you wanted to see?' I asked when we were back outside.

She smiled, a shade coquettishly. 'Is there anything else you think I should see?'

'There is, as a matter of fact,' I said, remembering Dr

Fitzpatrick's request. 'The Occupational Health and Safety department.'

She gave a snort. 'I'd say there was a contradiction in terms there somewhere, wouldn't you?'

'No, I wouldn't.' I looked at her. 'It was you at the Holfords' house last week, wasn't it?'

'Yes. And wasn't it rather insensitive of *you* to be there at that time?'

'I was Steve's boss. I wanted to tell him I was sorry, and to offer him help. I didn't think Jane would be there. Is she at home now?'

'She's due to go back home tomorrow, after a few days in hospital.' She paused. 'We've decided not to have her back on the picket. On medical advice.'

'I'm glad about that. I don't think that was very sensitive, either.'

'It was her decision,' she said sharply, defensively.

'Still not very sensitive.'

She looked away. 'Perhaps not,' she said, after a pause.

'Come.'

Fitzpatrick always uttered the word in a tone that made it sound more like Go. I pushed the door open.

He looked up from his desk. 'Hello. What do you want?'

'David Rossily told me you'd asked to meet the representative from WANT.'

'Oh yes,' he said in a different tone as he got to his feet.

'Won't you both sit down?' he said after I'd introduced them.

We sat.

'I asked to see you,' he began carefully, addressing Sarah, 'because part of my job is to correlate all the information gathered in our environmental monitoring programme. I thought you'd be interested to see the results.'

'Er—yes,' said Sarah guardedly.

'We began before the station became operational by

taking a very large number of samples within a thirty-mile radius to establish the naturally occurring radiation levels. All subsequent results have been compared with those levels.'

'What sort of samples do you take?' Sarah asked.

'Milk, grass and soil from the land; seaweed, silt and marine life from the sea. These are taken from fixed points at fixed intervals.'

'What about sea-water, air?'

'Those too, of course, only more frequently. Daily, in fact. But sea-water and air samples can only show whether radiation has escaped. The grass and seaweed samples are more sensitive, since they show whether radiation has been absorbed over a period of time.'

'I see. So now you're going to tell me that there's been no increase whatsoever over the background level since you started.' She smiled at him. 'Aren't you?'

He smiled back. 'Correct. And that's been confirmed by both the Department of the Environment, and the Ministry of Ag, Fish and Food.'

'Who are, of course, completely disinterested Government departments.'

'They are not disinterested, as we both know. They have a very strong interest in ensuring that we *don't* release any radiation.'

Sarah paused, then said, 'So how do you explain the increase in childhood leukæmia in this area. Or in other areas where there are nuclear installations? These increases are accepted facts, aren't they?'

'Indeed they are.' He got up from his seat and went over to the map on the wall. 'The other areas being here, at Sellafield, and also here, at Dounreay in Scotland.'

'You said it, doctor. So how do you explain it?'

'Well, Professor Gardner at Southampton University has suggested that the Sellafield cases are caused by the comparatively small doses of radiation, ten millisieverts or more, received by the fathers during the six months before conception of the children.'

'I couldn't have put it better myself,' said Sarah.

'But there are many men at Sellafield who have received much larger doses than that and have not fathered leukæmic children.'

She shrugged. 'Some people are more susceptible than others. I thought that was accepted medical knowledge.'

'So it is. But nobody here at Somerset Nuclear Electric receives anything like ten millisieverts.'

'Then I suggest that either your measurements are wrong, or, more likely, that even the smallest doses of radiation, below your thresholds, can give rise to leukæmia. What other explanation is there?'

'I'm very glad you asked me that.' He smiled a slightly predatory smile. 'Other explanations, let's see now. Well, there's radon gas, emitted from granite and certain other rocks—'

'I thought radon caused lung cancer, not leukæmia. Besides, I don't think there are any radon-emitting rocks around Sellafield.'

'Perhaps not, although there is bracken.'

'Bracken?'

'Yes. The stuff that looks like fern and tends to grow in the sort of places nuclear power stations are built. And it's been proved to cause cancer.'

'So now you're trying to tell me it's all down to bracken?'

'Researchers at the University of Wales seem to think so, but no, I'm not so sure. I mention these things just to give you an idea of just how many possibilities there are.'

'So what's your theory, doctor?' She spoke with an edge to her voice. 'From your tone, I feel sure you must have one.'

'Not a theory of my own, no. I tend to favour that of Dr Kinlen and his team at the Cancer Research Campaign's unit in Oxford University.'

'And that is?'

'You agree that there's been a significant increase in childhood leukæmia here, and at Sellafield and Dounreay?'

'Of course.'

'Similar significant increases have also been found over the last forty years in several rural new towns around Britain. Note that, *rural*.'

'Which new towns?'

He moved back to the map. 'Aycliffe and Peterlee, here in the north-east.' He pointed. 'Glenrothes in Scotland, Cwmbran in Wales, and Corby in Northants. And there are no nuclear installations anywhere near any of those places.'

'Has this data been published?'

'Yes, in the *Lancet*. Would you like the reference?'

Sarah pulled out her notebook. 'Please.'

He gave it to her, then continued, 'Childhood leukæmia is almost certainly the rare outcome of a viral infection, and those towns have all had large influxes of young couples with children, which has upset the epidemiological balance. In these towns, and also in areas such as Sellafield and this area, it is the influx of a diverse young population that has led to more of the virus being transmitted. This, in turn, has led to the increase in childhood leukæmia.'

'Why did you emphasize just now that these towns are rural?'

'Because areas like Sellafield are epidemiologically very similar. In the new towns of a more metropolitan nature, Bracknell or Basildon, for instance, where the people are of less diverse origin, there has been no significant increase in childhood leukæmia.'

She hesitated, drew in a breath. 'Doctor, how much of this has been actually proved?'

He smiled. 'That depends on how you define proof. It is accepted that the majority of childhood leukæmia is caused by a virus. The epidemiological theory is sound, and I find the data convincing.'

'But others may not,' said Sarah, snapping shut her notebook. 'However, we shall certainly look into it. Was there anything else you wanted to tell me before I go?'

'Yes, Ms Brierly, there was.' He resumed his seat and leaned forward, facing her. 'I didn't tell you all this in order to score points. Your organization hasn't a hope of winning the Holford case, as I suspect your principals know very well. Persuade them to give it up, *please*. It's not doing anyone any good, and it's doing the Holfords a great deal of harm. That's all.'

'I shall certainly pass your views on,' Sarah said. 'Thank you, doctor, and goodbye.'

'Goodbye, Ms Brierly.'

Outside, she took a deep breath and slowly released it.

'Is there anything else I can show you?' I asked, after a pause.

'Thank you, no,' she replied, rather formally. 'Other than the way back to the gate.'

'OK.'

We walked in silence. This was probably my last chance of speaking to her alone . . .

'Didn't you say yesterday you wanted to look at the inlet and outlet of the sea-water cooling system?'

'Well, I certainly don't want to see those drum screen things again, thank you very much.' She paused. 'But I ought to look at the outlet, I suppose. Will it take very long?'

'No.'

We walked in silence. I took her over to a circular wall, about four feet high and a hundred feet across.

'My God!' she said reverently as she looked over. 'I had no idea you used so much water.'

Fifty feet below was a mælstrom created by twin torrents surging into a basin to drain into the sea.

She brought out her camera. 'What d'you call this?'

'The Seal Pit.'

She took a couple of shots. 'What would happen if you fell in?'

'You'd be very quickly killed and washed out to sea.'

She looked up. 'Has that ever happened?'

I shook my head.

'Where does it enter the sea?'

'Over there.' I pointed. 'Where the red markers are.'

She gazed for a little, then said, 'All that hot water going into the sea, doesn't it have an effect on the local ecology?'

I grinned. 'Indeed it does. The local anglers tell us that the fish here grow fifty per cent bigger. It attracts the bird life too. The whole area's a nature reserve.'

She made no comment on this, but said, 'Can you get down to the beach from here? I'd like a shot of the rig, if possible.' A strand of hair escaped and she impatiently pushed it back.

'Sure.'

We walked down past the workshops and storage huts and along the perimeter fence to the gate. Although the sun was still warm, it was a cool, fresh day for late summer, thanks to the brisk sou'westerly breeze. Stately cumulus rode the sky, white horses the water, and you could see across the channel to Wales.

I found my card key, pushed it into the socket and pulled the gate open.

'Isn't this gate a bit of a security risk?' she asked as she followed me through.

'Not really, since a light goes on in Security when it's used. We're installing close circuit cameras, this week, I think, to tighten it up. Why, thinking of breaking in?'

'Maybe.' She smiled as she said it; she seemed to have recovered her humour.

I smiled back and led her past the row of tamarisks that grew outside the fence, up the steps cut into the sea-wall and down the other side where the dinghy rested rather forlornly on the shingle. A concrete path led down through the rocks to the water, wide enough to trail the dinghy along if necessary.

We started walking towards the sea. The concrete was specially roughened so that it wasn't slippery, even when wet. The tide was about two hundred yards out.

She said, 'The sea-water inlet's under the rig, right?'

'Right.'

'But what's the rig actually for? Why d'you need the crane?'

'Maintenance. Unblocking the inlet, if the need arose.'

'Has it ever been blocked?'

'No.'

The sea was slapping against the sides of the path. She stopped and took several photos, then lowered the camera.

'Where's the nature reserve you were talking about?'

'Over there, where the estuary comes into the bay.' I pointed. 'When the tide goes out, it leaves acres and acres of mud, full of tasty delicacies for the waders.'

'I'd rather not dwell on that,' she said with a shudder. 'That's obviously Wales over there . . . So what's the head-land down there, where it dips into the sea?'

'Northhead.'

'Really? Of Butlin's fame?'

I nodded.

'But it's beautiful, you feel there must be something there better than Northhead.'

It's a view I'm used to, but it did look good that day, the outlines of Wales, the headlands and islands sharply pointed. Almost exotic . . .

Even the sea looked good. Usually it's the colour of draught Guinness, because of all the mud sloshing round the basin in the tides, but today, it had a reddish tint, set off by the white horses and the foam of the waves that gurgled and muttered among the wasteland of rock and swirling bladderwrack.

'Whereabouts is Exmoor from here?' she asked. 'Those hills beyond Northhead?'

'Yes, that's part of it. In fact, the nearest bit of authentic moorland is on the headland you were looking at, above Northhead.'

She turned to me. 'How d'you mean, authentic moorland?'

'Heathermoor. A lot of the heather on Exmoor has been ploughed up now, but North Hill still has a fair amount.'

'Being where it is, I imagine it's pretty well inundated with tourists this time of year.'

'Around the car park at the far end, yes, but otherwise you can usually find a bit to yourself.'

Her eyes went back to the headland. There would never be a better chance. I said, 'I'll show you if you like. This evening.'

She turned to me again, amusement in her eyes. 'What is this? Fraternizing with the enemy?'

I smiled back. 'You can call it that.'

Her eyes grew serious. 'Don't try and involve me, Michael. It wouldn't work.'

'Isn't that my lookout?'

After an age, she said, 'All right, your lookout. What time?'

'Seven?'

'All right,' she said again. 'Seven. At the Queen's Head.'

David was just coming out of my office as I got back.

'Ah, Michael—is *Mizz* Brierly still with you?'

'No. I left her at the gate about five minutes—'

'Damn! You'd better come with me,' he said grimly.

'What's happened, David?' I said, following him back to his office.

'Only that the bitch has done the very thing she was told not to—leaked the story of Don to the press.'

CHAPTER 8

It was in the early edition of the *Western Evening News*. David thrust the paper into my hands and lit a cigarette as I read it.

MYSTERY OF NUKE ENGINEER'S BODY

The body of 38-year-old engineer Donald Waterford was found yesterday at Somerset Nuclear Electric, better known locally as Desolation Point. The body was discovered in the Drum Screen Pits by an as yet unnamed member of WANT (Women Against Nuclear Technology, the pressure group offshoot of the Greenham Common Women that is at present picketing the power station). She was on a fact-finding tour of the station.

This tragedy, following so closely on the equally tragic death of Liam Holford last week from leukæmia, can only be further bad news for the beleaguered power station, which has had a controversial history since it was opened some fifteen years ago.

('What bloody controversy?' demanded David.)

When we telephoned the station earlier today, a spokesman refused to comment . . .

('Lies, bloody lies,' spluttered David.)

. . . and the police would only confirm that father of two Donald Waterford's body had been found on the site of the station.

Elizabeth Tregenna, Chairperson of WANT, told us late yesterday that this latest death only confirmed the pressure group's worst fears.

'Whether this unfortunate man's death was due to radiation is irrelevant,' she declared. 'Nuclear power stations are dangerous places and the sooner the public grasps this fact the better.

'It is indeed fortunate that it was one of our members who made the discovery; otherwise, would this tragic death have been made public?'

WANT are providing financial backing for Mr and Mrs Holford, who claim that their son's leukæmia was caused by the effect of radiation on Mr Holford before Liam's conception . . .

There was more in the same vein.

'The only bad news is this paper itself,' fumed David.

'Did they or didn't they telephone this morning?' I asked.

'No they bloody didn't, but there's no way of proving that. The point is,' he continued, rounding on me, 'that Mizz bloody Brierly has got to be behind this, hasn't she?'

'Has she?'

'Who else could it be?'

'Some of the staff must have had an idea—'

'Not in that amount of detail. Besides, it explains why she was in such a hurry to have the rest of her guided tour, doesn't it? To do it before this got out.'

'That's circumstantial. Besides—'

'Like it was circumstantial you happened to run into her last night? She's certainly got you taped, hasn't she, sunshine?'

I felt myself colour, which on top of the irritation (intended) that being called sunshine always elicited, only made me even more angry.

'You have no proof, David, and therefore no right to

make that kind of accusation about her. Or that kind of innuendo about me.'

Our eyes locked, his mouth trembled and I was sure we were in for a row and wasn't sorry, then he abruptly changed his mind.

'OK, Michael, I shouldn't have made that crack about you.' His voice hardened. 'But you'll not easily convince me that Mizz Brierly wasn't behind this.' He slapped the newspaper down on his desk.

So what the hell am I supposed to do about my date tonight? I wondered, back in my own office. Because in spite of what I'd said to David, it was beginning to look as though Sarah had seen me coming.

'What's the matter, Michael?'

I turned to see Rhiannon standing in the open doorway. I didn't know how long she'd been there.

'Nothing. Just thinking.'

'Well,' she said, coming into the office, 'I wouldn't want to see your face when there *was* something.'

'A slight altercation with David, if you must know.'

'And I thought you were such great pals.'

I smiled. 'David's all right. It's those bloody women—' I indicated the perimeter fence with my thumb—'they're getting him down. Not to mention Don being killed.'

She moved past me to the window as though she hadn't heard.

'Those bloody women,' she murmured. 'Yes.' She turned back on me suddenly.

'I wish you wouldn't speak about them like that. It makes you sound stereotyped, which you're not.'

'That's—'

'Those women . . . I don't agree with them, but they are being women, aren't they? D'you remember you once said to me that women are closer to the earth than men? Well, those women believe that what we are doing is spoiling the earth, souring it for future generations, so they're challenging us to prove otherwise. Is that such a bad thing?'

'Not when you put it like that, no, but—'

'Then please don't talk about those women the way you were. It's beneath you.'

'OK, lesson absorbed.' I paused. 'I'm sure that isn't what you came here for . . .'

'No. Two things. First, Brian Cleveland's been telling my crew that there's something wrong with the Arkell hoist and they're worried about it. Is there or isn't there anything wrong with the Arkell?'

'There isn't. Brian's got a fixation about it for some reason. We'll both go down now, if you like, and put a stop to it. What was the other thing?'

'You haven't forgotten you were going to give me a hand with the Hymek tonight?'

Her diesel. I closed my eyes and put my hand to my forehead . . .

'I can see you have,' she continued resignedly.

My mind raced. I knew I ought to cancel my date with Sarah, but I couldn't.

'I'm sorry, Rhiannon, but something's come up and I can't make it tonight.'

She sighed. 'I won't say just like a man, although it is. Let's go and sort out Brian, shall we?'

She was making light of it, but I could see she was hurt. I stood up and followed her to the door.

I'd better explain about Rhiannon.

She's our Woman Engineer, a Charge Engineer, the same grade as me. Women are doing as well as men in all sorts of professions these days, better in some cases, but women engineers still aren't all that common, especially at that grade.

She'd come to us three years before, straight from university, where she'd got a good 2/1 degree in mechanical engineering.

She doesn't look like an engineer. She's tall, five feet eight, and slim—some might say too slim, her figure on the borderline between grace and awkwardness. She has short, very dark red hair, enormous blue eyes like lamps and a face shaped by her high cheekbones. Dear-like is perhaps the best way to describe her. Doe-like.'

She's Welsh—has to be with a name like hers—from Gower, and with the pretty accent they seem to breed there. She's introvert in some ways, but also absolutely determined to succeed, which is why she acquired so fearsome a reputation in her first year here. She had to be pretty ruthless with some of the blokes she was in charge of, hence the whispers about her being sexless, which simply isn't true.

And how do I know that?

Well, one day, a few months after she arrived, we were talking in the coffee lounge together and she asked me about the engineering work I sometimes did for the West Somerset Railway, the preserved line that runs to Northhead. I told her about it and suggested she come along, which she did. A few months later she was in charge of a project to restore the Hymek, a big mainline diesel, and now, nearly two years after that, the work was almost finished. Determination and organizing skill.

About a year ago they'd held a party at Lydeard when one of the other projects was finished. It was just after Julia had left me and I went along feeling rather sorry for myself. I drank too much. Rhiannon was there. I chatted to her, brightly, enthusiastically—I just wanted a woman to talk to.

I asked her how the Hymek was coming along, suggested we take a look. Drinks in hand, we sauntered over in the warm evening air and admired it; long, green, powerful, with yellow warning flashes on the front. We climbed into the cab.

It was filled with old-fashioned smells, leather, brass, oil.

I wasn't paying much attention to what she was saying; she'd suddenly become overwhelmingly attractive. I slid my arms around her waist from behind and nuzzled her neck. The material of her dress was thin and I could feel the life flowing in her skin underneath.

She turned and we kissed and after a time, I slid my hands into her dress. Her breasts were like small, firm fruit.

She opened her eyes, swallowed and said, 'Isn't it too soon, Michael? For you, I mean.'

'No.'

Nobody could see us in the diesel.

She said, 'I don't mess around, Michael,' which should have warned me.

Instead I said, fatuously, 'Neither do I.'

I'd have taken her there and then, but she stopped me.

She said nervously, uncertainly, 'Your place or mine?'

She lived not far away, so we went there and made love, or at least, she did. I do remember being surprised by her sheer sexuality.

I avoided her for a week after that. Eventually, she cornered me in my office.

'Why are you avoiding me, Michael?'

'You know why.'

'Tell me.'

'I'm ashamed of myself. I used you.'

'I could have said no. I knew what I was doing.'

'I'm still not very proud of myself.'

'That has to be your problem. Meanwhile, we're colleagues, we have to work together, so I suggest that if we can't be friendly, we're at least civil.'

I looked into her lamplike eyes. 'You're right. I'm sorry.'

'Shake on it?'

'Sure.'

The trouble is, no matter how you rationalize it, however civilized you may be, once you've known someone sexually,

your relationship can never be quite the same. Add to that
the fact that, however prettily you dress it up, I'd turned
her down. Tried the goods and rejected them.

But we did remain on civil, if not friendly terms and
recently our relationship had become warmer.

But that, unfortunately, was the Old Adam at work. I'd
allowed myself to become drawn to her and my body had
told me that she was there for the taking. I'd been on the
point of letting it happen when the Gorgeous One, Sarah,
had appeared and I'd put on the brakes and let her down
again.

I was about to go down with her now and take it out on
Brian when Rod burst in.

'Michael, quick, it's Steve—he's trying to bugger up the
turbine . . .'

CHAPTER 9

I followed him at a run. 'Where is he now?'

'On top of number three turbine—this way, Darren's
holding the lift.'

I followed him inside.

'Wait!' shouted Rhiannon from behind us.

Darren stabbed the button as soon as she was inside; the
doors closed, the lift jerked.

'What happened?' I asked Rod.

'I saw him on top of the oil tank. I was goin' to speak
to him, say sorry, like, then I saw he had the filler lid off
and was puttin' somethin' inside. I runs up to 'im, says,
What you doin'?—then 'e 'its me, 'ere.' He pointed to a
mark on his jaw.

'What was he putting into the tank?'

'Grinding paste.'

'Oh, Jesus wept!'

I ran out of the lift as the doors opened, along the passage and out on to the steel gallery that ran around the perimeter of the Turbine Hall. The noise enveloped me—no time to worry about ear muffs now . . .

I turned right, on to the gangway to number three, then stopped by the oil tank that fed both the turbine and generator systems. The filler plate was off and a large can of grinding paste stood open beside it . . .

Should I have the turbine shut down, or risk letting it run?

How much paste had gone in? I picked up the can. Not much. Had he actually got *any* in there? Would the filters stop it before it reached the bearings?

To shut down the turbine now would mean a Scram, and that was to be avoided at all . . . if at all possible.

'Where is he?' I shouted.

'Up there.' Rod pointed to the top of the turbine. Steve was standing on the tiny platform next to the top condenser, holding an iron bar. Two blokes stood at the bottom of the ladder looking up at him.

I turned to Darren. 'Go and fetch Doc Fitzpatrick, now. Tell him what's happened. Rhiannon, could you—?'

'I'm coming with you.'

'No, he's—'

'He might listen to me.'

He might, at that. 'All right. Rod, you go and find out whether the oil filter in here will hold the grinding paste back.'

I walked quickly along the gangway beside the generator. Thirty feet below, white faces stared up.

Up the steps, along the catwalk to the iron ladder leading up to the condenser.

'Back!' I yelled at the two blokes standing there. They nodded, dropped back. Steve looked down at me, his lips moving.

'Let me,' shouted Rhiannon in my ear. I nodded.

She began climbing the ladder. Steve shouted something, brandished the iron bar. Still she climbed, trying to speak to him as she did . . . She was banking on him not hitting *her*.

Suddenly he jumped back, still holding the bar, climbed the railings that surrounded the platform.

Rhiannon's head reached the level of the platform . . .

'Steve, *no!*' I heard her scream, then she quickly came back down the ladder. Steve stayed where he was.

'He said he was going to jump unless I went back,' she shouted at me.

I looked up. He'd brought one leg back over the railings now, so that now he was straddling them, still holding the bar. I looked over my shoulder—no sign of Fitzpatrick yet.

To talk to him, or not to talk to him . . . ?

I'd been on the point of breaking through to him that day at his house before Jane came back, I was sure . . .

I began climbing the ladder. He was out of sight. The rungs were slippery, or was that just my imagination? I had no idea of what he was doing until my head came level with the platform—when it might meet an iron bar coming the other way. Or the sight of him falling from the rails . . .

I stopped. Felt lonely.

But nothing to what he must be feeling, I thought, and went on.

No sound, just the shriek of the steam as it tore through the turbines.

One more step.

My eyes came over the level of the platform . . . no sign of him.

'Get back, Michael!'

I looked up to see him sitting on the rounded top of the condenser, clinging to the vacuum gauge.

'Please,' I shouted. 'I just want to talk.' I moved up three rungs as I said this.

'Get back!'

'I've got some news for you, Steve, good news.' Two more steps.

Uncertainty crossed his face. 'What?'

'About Jane.' Another step. 'She's going to be all right.' I was on the platform.

'Jane's never goin' to be all right,' he screamed. He pushed himself back and brought the iron bar down on to the vacuum gauge, smashing it and nearly over-balancing . . .

Oh Christ, I thought profanely as the whistle made by the hole as it sucked in air told me I had about ten minutes to talk him down and block it, before all the vacuum was lost and we went into Scram.

The whites went all the way round his eyes. He trembled all over.

'It's true,' I shouted. 'One of the WANT people told me just now. They're discharging her tomorrow.'

'I know that,' he shouted back. 'But she's never gonna be all right 'cos we can't have any more kids, that's what's wrong with her.'

'But you can!' My throat felt raw already. 'Doc Fitz-patrick told me earlier today. It's a virus that gave Liam leukæmia, not this place.'

'You're lying!'

'It's been scientifically proved, I swear it.' Bending the truth slightly, but forgivable. 'He'll tell you himself in a minute.'

Then I sensed a movement on the periphery of my sight —someone, Darren, had gone up to the catwalk that went along the top of the turbine and was creeping up behind him . . .

Steve saw the movement in my eyes and looked round, swiped with the bar and overbalanced, slipping down the turbine's smooth, painted surface.

He fell in slow motion, his arms striking the railing—

then self-preservation took over and his fingers clutched as I grabbed handfuls of overall. He held . . .

I looked past his eyes to the floor fifty feet below and said, 'Pull, Steve.'

We both pulled and very slowly his head came over the top of the rail, his foot found a purchase, then he was over and we fell in a heap on the platform.

By the time Fitzpatrick found us, he was crying while I held him and said over and over, 'It's true, Steve, I swear it's true . . .'

Fitzpatrick persuaded David not to involve the police, since it would only make Steve's condition worse. He then arranged for him to be treated for shock in hospital over-night, and for him and Jane then to stay with Jane's parents in Bristol for a time. This, he said, would keep them out of mischief as well as give them a change of surroundings.

Steve hadn't managed to get any of the paste into the oil tank.

CHAPTER 10

Sarah was waiting for me outside the Queen's Head and got into the car with a smile as I opened the door.

'Thanks. It's years since I've been in an open-topped car.' She was wearing pink cotton jeans and a white top and looked absolutely terrific, which made it harder saying what I had to say.

'Before we go, there's something I have to ask you—two things.'

She made it worse by pretending to look solemn.

'Oh dear,' she said. 'Do I have to pass a test before I'm allowed out with you?'

I handed her the copy of the *Western Evening News* I'd

bought on the way home. 'Did you know about this article?'

She glanced at it and looked up. 'I . . . had been warned that something might be coming out, yes.'

'Did you leak it?'

'No. I told the cops I wouldn't, and I didn't.'

'Who did, then?'

'I don't know.' She paused. 'Besides, does it matter all that much? It would've had to have been reported at some stage.'

'It's the timing. Bad timing, from our point of view.'

'Yes, I can see that, but doesn't it rather underline our basic conflict of interests? Already, you don't know whether to believe me. I did warn you.'

'OK, so I believe you, but that's not all.'

'Well?'

'Steve Holford came into the station this afternoon and was caught trying to sabotage one of the turbines.'

She closed her eyes. 'Oh no.'

'Yes. He's in hospital now, but the thing is—'

'Michael, WANT is completely non-violent. If we'd had any idea, we'd have done everything we could to prevent it. Could you tell me exactly what happened, please?'

I gave her an edited version and she opened the car door. 'I must tell Liz. I won't be a minute.'

She was back within three.

'Liz already knew about it. She rang the hospital and offered to bring him home tomorrow, but he's already made other arrangements.'

'How did she know about it?'

'I don't know,' she said quickly. 'Maybe Jane told her. Shall we go?'

I started the engine and drove away.

Neither of us spoke for a while, then, as we crested a hill overlooking the channel, she said, 'Is there a coast road we can follow?'

'Not just here. This stretch of the coast was never built up.'

'Thus, Desolation Point.'

A little further along, the road does touch the sea in places.

At Watchport, where a largish cargo ship was being unloaded and another was manœuvring out of the harbour on the tide.

'I didn't realize it was a working port,' she said. 'Can we stop for a moment?'

As I pulled in by the harbour front, a fat and elderly character in a seaman's cap materialized beside us.

'Can't park there, midear—Oh, 'ello, Michael, didn' recognize you . . .'

'A couple of minutes, Walter, OK?'

'All right, midear, but no more, mind.' He winked at Sarah.

'He's priceless,' she said, as we walked along the harbour wall. 'How come you know him?'

'I keep a dinghy here. I know most of the people who work round the harbour.'

'Oh. Can anyone keep a boat here?' she asked, looking at the mixture of fishing and pleasure boats.

'Anyone can moor temporarily, for a fee. There's a waiting list for permanent berths.'

She turned her attention back to the cargo ship as it cleared the lighthouse at the harbour entrance.

'What's that black motorboat doing?'

'It's the pilot vessel. The ship drops the pilot a little way out and the pilot vessel brings him back.'

'Can we watch?'

'Better not.' I nodded to where Walter was waiting.

We drove on through Blue Water Bay, which belies its name save for an hour or so on a clear day when the tide covers up the mud, and thence to Northhead, tourist overspill town of the west, packed with T-shirts bearing legends such as *Smeg-head* and *I Love Love Lager Louts*.

I found the road which looks like a side-street, but leads up to the Old Town.

'Stop a minute, Michael, this is lovely.'

I pulled up by the church, opposite which a cobbled alleyway wound down through a group of cottages so old they seemed to have grown from the rock.

She turned to me. 'It's hard to believe it's the same place, isn't it?'

'Yes.'

After a moment I drove out of the town and up through the wooded hairpins leading to North Hill.

Oddly enough, August, a flat month generally for the English countryside, is one of Exmoor's best. The heather's at its most riotous purple, interspersed with yellow gorse and patches of cotton grass rippling like wheat in the breeze.

'I'll drive to the end of the road,' I said. 'Then we'll come back a little way for a walk, if you like.'

'You can drive along here for ever,' she said dreamily.

The little road fits so snugly into the contours and is so smooth that we seemed to be floating through the colours.

There were about two score cars in the park at the end and as many people straggled along the path to the cliffs. The curve of Dorlock Bay lay a thousand feet below while across the vale, the moor beneath the westering sun was black and changeless.

After a few minutes I turned the car and drove about half way back along the road before pulling off.

'Would you like to walk a little way?'

'Mmm.'

She got out and wandered over to a wooden signpost while I pulled the tonneau over the car.

'What's this?' she asked, indicating the signpost. 'Burgundy Chapel.'

'It's a chapel, or what's left of one, built by the Burgundian monks.'

'Is it far?'

'No. It's steep, though. Want to have a look?'

'Why not?'

We set off.

'I don't call this steep,' she said a few minutes later.

'You wait.'

A few more minutes later, she said, 'I see what you mean.'

'Want to go back?'

She looked down at her trainers which were covered in dust where she'd slithered down a particularly sharp gradient.

'No, we might as well go on now.'

We reached the chapel about ten minutes later. Although there's not much of it left, one corner, including part of the door, is quite well preserved.

'Look at this arch,' she said, running her finger over the dressed stone. 'They must have carved the pieces and brought them down by mule. Did they have mules in those days? How old is it, anyway?'

'About five hundred years, I think. I don't know about mules. They'd have had donkeys, though.'

'And look at this.' She was running her fingers over the rough stones of the exterior. 'Look how each stone has been shaped so that the edges are all in line with each other. It's a work of love.'

We stayed a few more minutes absorbing the atmosphere, then started back.

We were about half way up when she stopped, her face glowing. 'I'm going to have to get my breath back a minute.'

The thickly gorsed sides of the combe surrounded us with its silence.

She said suddenly, 'I'll bet the ship we saw leaving the harbour gives that a wide berth.'

She was looking down at the foreshore. Although the water was still high, the troughs between the waves exposed the toothed edges of the rocks that ran some way out to sea.

'Not exactly a welcoming landfall, is it?'

'To say the least.'

By the time we reached the top, the sun had lost its power and was sinking, a deep orange, into the sea. There was a fresh breeze, and we stood in it for a while, cooling off.

She said slowly, 'I'll say this for it, the coastline's better here than at Desolation Point. But I think I still prefer Cornwall, or Dorset.'

'I know what you mean.' I hesitated. 'I like it here because it's the only place I know where you can . . . see where you are. See the whole country.'

She turned to me. 'How do you mean?'

'Well, you know what Britain looks like on a map, but it's still only lines on paper.' She was still looking at me, so I tried to gather my thoughts.

'You can see Wales over there, and believe that the coast goes all the way along to Milford Haven. You can imagine this coast going round North Devon and into Cornwall, and the Severn going all the way up to Gloucester. And from there, you can believe that there's a place called the Wash a couple of hundred miles north-east of that . . . You can see the whole country . . . or at least, I can,' I finished lamely.

'I've never thought of it like that.' She studied the horizons. 'I *think* I can see it, although it takes a bit of a mental leap.'

After a short silence, she said, 'Where would the hydro-electric barrage go, if it were built?'

'There's a sort of neck up there—' I pointed—'from

Weston-super-Mare over to Barry, which is about eight
miles across. Or it might be nearer Bristol, where it's
narrower.'

'Would it bother you? You love it here, don't you?'

I smiled. 'No, and yes. Shall we go back to the car?'

'All right.'

The heather made the faintest ringing noise as it
scratched against our feet.

I said, 'The main thing I've got against the barrage is
that it would cost about fifteen billion to build, and yet
produce no more electricity than Somerset Nuclear Electric,
which only cost about three billion in today's money.'

'But once built, it would produce an infinite supply of
pollution free, *safe* electricity.'

'And devastate the winter feeding grounds of the wildfowl
from here to Slimbridge.'

'That has yet to be proved,' she said.

'The only way to prove it would be to build the damn
thing and see,' I retorted.

She sighed. 'I wonder if we ought to keep off this subject.'

'Perhaps you're right.'

We walked a little way in silence, then she turned to me
and said, 'Just to change the subject, *is* there such a thing
as the Exmoor Beast?'

'Well, there's something. There've been too many sight-
ings, not to mention sheep killed, for it to be put down to
imagination.' I grinned at her. 'Don't worry, we're not
likely to run into one of them here.'

'I'm not worried. Much.' She glanced quickly behind.
'You said one of them. One of what?'

'Some kind of puma, probably. Quite a few were illegally
released in this country over the years, and Exmoor's an
ideal place for them.'

'Why?'

'It's full of nooks and crannies for them to hide in. Like
the combe we've just been down, for instance.'

'If you'd told me that earlier, I wouldn't have gone.'

We reached the car and I unzipped it.

'Were you born round here?' she asked.

'Yes. Why? Does it show?'

'It does, a bit.'

'In what way?' I asked, curious.

'Your accent, you've got a slight burr. Your local knowledge. And your . . . your horizons. And don't ask me to explain that.'

I hesitated, then said, 'I'll buy you a drink instead.'

'All right. I don't want to be back late, though.'

There aren't many truly rural pubs left in southern England, but the one I took her to a little way out of Northhead isn't bad. There were even a couple of farmers there as well as a sprinkling of locals and tourists.

'What would you like?' I asked.

'Oh, a glass of beer, please.'

I bought a pint for myself and took them over to where she was sitting.

She took a mouthful, murmured, 'Mm, nice,' and put the glass down. 'Well, whatever shall we talk about if power stations are verboten?'

'We'll talk about you, if you like. Where do you live?'

'London.'

'Ooh ah, London. Big place. I went there once, you know.'

'Streatham.'

'Oh, I know, where they have the race riots.'

'That's Brixton, you idiot. Would you rather talk about you?'

'No.' I drank some beer. 'Are you married?'

'Divorced. One daughter, Sally, aged five, at present with my parents.'

'I'm sorry.'

'You needn't be, he was a louse. This isn't what we want to talk about, is it, Michael?'

It was a strange thing for her to say, especially after wanting the subject closed earlier, and yet she was right. We somehow needed to justify ourselves to each other.

'Were you at Greenham Common?' I asked.

'Yes, I was, for a short while.'

'Have you always felt that strongly?'

'No, it didn't bother me much when I was younger.' She fumbled in her bag, took out a cigarette and lit it with a bijou lighter.

'I didn't know you smoked.'

'The time hasn't quite come yet when we have to wear a badge saying: Beware, Smoker.' She took a puff. 'As I was saying, or about to say, what changed me was a radio play I heard some years ago based on Raymond Briggs's book *When the Wind Blows*. Did you ever hear it?'

I shook my head.

'It's about this absurdly patriotic old couple after a nuclear attack. They get radiation sickness and die, slowly, and yet never lose their faith in the Government.' She drew on her cigarette again. 'It made me weep. And I mean, really cry.' She took another nervous puff, remembering.

'I believe you,' I said, looking at her. 'Nuclear power stations aren't the same as nuclear weapons, though.'

'That didn't stop Chernobyl killing all those people. Or the tens, maybe hundreds, of thousands who will die from radiation-induced cancers. I don't suppose we'll never know the final total.'

'You're absolutely right. Which is why, when over forty years ago that type of reactor was considered for use in this country, it was rejected as being fundamentally flawed—'

'I know all that. You told me all that before,' she said, her hands slicing downwards and making a zigzag of cigarette smoke. 'But it doesn't help Liam Holford, does it?'

'Liam's beyond our help,' I said. 'It's Steve and Jane who need help now. And WANT isn't helping them.'

'That's a matter of opinion.'

'Didn't what Dr Fitzpatrick said today mean anything to you?'

She took a last puff on her cigarette, then carefully stubbed it out. 'To tell you the truth,' she said, 'I don't know. He may or may not be right about that particular case, but that doesn't alter the fact that nuclear technology is fundamentally dangerous and must be stopped.'

'So as far as the Holfords go, the end justifies the means?'

'That's hardly fair,' she began angrily.

The door threw open and Rhiannon came in, accompanied by John Burton and two others. She saw me immediately and smiled.

'Hello, Michael, you didn't say . . .' Then she took in Sarah. 'Oh, I see.'

She turned quickly and made for the bar and John, after giving me a reproving, but not unhappy look, followed.

CHAPTER 11

'What an extraordinary girl,' said Sarah. She looked at me quizzically. 'Michael, did you stand her up so that you could take me out?'

'No, I didn't,' I said in a low voice, protesting a shade much. 'She's a colleague and we had a loose arrangement that I'd try and give her a hand with something. To tell you the truth, I'd forgotten all about it until she reminded me late this afternoon.'

'Hmm. I have this feeling you've upset her quite a lot. What were you going to give her a hand with?'

'You won't believe it, but repairing a diesel locomotive.'

'What, a railway engine? Are you train buffs?'

'She's the head of a team that's rebuilt a diesel engine. I sometimes do some engineering work on one of the steam engines. She happened to want me along tonight for some reason.'

'I've never come across a female train buff before,' she mused. 'Men, I can understand playing with trains, it's a retreat into childhood, but a woman . . .'

'Rhiannon's an engineer like me, and engineering is something that's total somehow, it's in your blood, to coin a cliché.' She didn't say anything, so I continued, 'It gives me a buzz, rebuilding a big engine, and Rhiannon feels the same about her diesel.'

She regarded me, nodding gently, then, with a start, looked at her watch.

'I wanted to be back by ten, and it's nearly that now.' She reached for her drink and finished it.

I did the same and we got up to go. I shot Rhiannon a guilty glance, but she was absorbed with her friends.

Outside, it was completely dark. I said, 'Would you like me to put the hood up?'

'Certainly not.'

We got in. As I fastened my seat-belt, I said, 'For all your talk, you haven't told me much about yourself. I don't even know what you do for a living. When you're not protesting, that is.'

'Guess.'

I started the engine. 'From your psychological insights and general mien, I'd say . . . a social worker.'

'Not bad. I'm a probation officer. When I'm not protesting. Now, home, please.'

There's nothing quite so sensuous as driving an open-topped car through a late summer night. I didn't try to talk, just enjoyed the scented night air and the feeling of floating through the darkness.

Outside the Queen's Head, she quickly opened the car door.

'Thanks for showing me round, Michael. It was fun.'

'Sarah . . . I'd like to see you again.'

'Doubtless you will.'

'That's not what I meant.'

'I know.' She leaned over and gave me the most fleeting of pecks. 'We'll see.'

I couldn't sleep that night and was consequently about ten minutes late the next morning. She was in her usual place when I drove in and gave me an enigmatic smile.

I hurried over to my office, trying to blink the grit out of my eyes. The phone was ringing as I walked in. I snatched it up.

'Michael Hempstead.'

'Ah, Michael.' David. 'Good of you to drop by.'

'I'm sorry, David, I overslept—'

'As our cousins would say, get your ass along here, fast.'

He'd made a joke of it, but he's not happy, I thought, hauling my ass along to his office.

Rhiannon, Peter and John were already there, also Kenny Parrish, Don's deputy, a small, neat man, with thinning hair and glasses.

'Sorry, David,' I said again as he waved me to a chair.

'You still look half asleep,' he said. 'Been on the tiles?'

I didn't reply (and Rhiannon didn't react, I noticed), so he went on, 'As I've been telling the others, we've got trouble. The radiation alarms on the cooling water for B circuit went off last night, and Kenny was called in. The monitors showed a peak of nearly a hundred MegaBecquerels, way over the limit. I've already contacted NII* and they should be here within the hour.'

'They haven't ordered us to shut down, then?'

'Not yet, although that could still happen.' He looked at the others. 'Have any of you still got the printout? Give it to Michael, will you?'

Wordlessly, Rhiannon handed it to me.

* Nuclear Installations Inspectorate.

'As you can see, there was just the one peak over about an hour last night. Nothing before, and virtually nothing after.'

'Do we know which isotopes were present yet?' I asked.

'Yes, and they're definitely from here.'

'Then why haven't NII—?'

'Shut us down?' David completed for me. 'Because I've persuaded them not to, although as I said earlier, they might when they get here.'

'I take it Sir knows about this.'

'Yes, and he's left it with me for the moment.' He paused. 'The thing is that NII already knew about this leak. They were about to telephone us, but I got there first, fortunately.'

'But how—' I began.

'It seems that our friends outside have started monitoring the cooling water outlet, and when they found this, they were on the phone to NII first thing this morning.'

'I'll bet they were,' said John.

David ignored him and continued: 'I've told them—NII, that is—that everything here is functioning perfectly, and suggested that it's something of a coincidence that WANT should just happen to be taking samples at the same time.'

'What did they say to that?'

'They didn't much like it,' said David carefully, 'but they do acknowledge the possibility. However, I think the main reason they've left us running is because if there *is* something wrong, it'll be easier to spot that way. And it's not as though the radiation was anywhere near danger level.'

We nodded our agreement.

'Before you came in, Michael, Kenny was going to tell us about the radiation levels picked up by the other sensors and in the routine samples taken at the time. Kenny?'

Kenny told us how the sensors in the boiler hadn't picked up any radiation at all, and that the routine samples taken from the cooling circuit either side of the condenser, and from the sea-water, had shown radiation peaks corresponding to that shown by the sensor inside the condenser.

'And that suggests to me,' David said, 'that someone, somehow, salted the cooling water for WANT to find.'

'But how could they have got the stuff into the system?' said John. 'Not the inlet, surely?'

'The Drum Screen Pit?' suggested Rhiannon.

There was an awkward little silence before David said, 'Could be, although it would mean that our security was compromised. Any point in taking samples from there now?'

'No,' said Peter abruptly. 'If there were any activity, it could just as easily have come from the contaminated sea-water.'

'Not if the level was higher,' said Rhiannon.

'OK, so we'll take samples,' said David quickly. 'We'll take them from anywhere we can think of. Can you organize that, please, Kenny? Anything else?'

'If you're right about WANT,' said John, 'how did they get hold of the material?'

'A good question,' said David. 'Any ideas, anyone?'

Peter said, 'Steve Holford is connected with WANT. Doesn't that make him the most likely culprit?' Peter was looking much worse than I could have done. His skin was papery, his voice trembled slightly and his shirt collar was dusted with dandruff. Strange how bald men still get dandruff.

'I don't see how,' said David, 'since he's been in hospital since yesterday afternoon.'

'Do you know that for a fact?'

'Yes, I do, because I phoned the hospital last night to ask about him. All right?'

'All right,' Peter said, after a pause.

'So, let's have a look at what else we know. The contamination certainly came from here, because of the isotope mixture. The single peak of radioactivity suggests to me a liquid, rather than a solid, which would have given a continuous level. And the most likely source of contaminated liquid would be the Cooling Ponds. Any problems with security down there, Peter?'

'No.'

'What about the body screening equipment, any problems there?'

'Look, what is this?' Peter burst out. 'Are you trying to suggest that I'm responsible for this?'

'Whatever gave you that—?'

'Because if you want to know, I've got an alibi for last night—'

'Peter, I'm just trying to look at all the possibilities, all right? Are there any problems with the body screening equipment?'

'None that I know of.' His voice had sunk almost to a whisper.

'Check, will you, please? Have any new staff started recently?'

'Er—yes, there is one.'

'Name?' David picked up a pen.

'Joanne Healey.'

He took a few details, then said, 'I'll have her checked out. Anything else?'

I said slowly, voicing the thoughts of the others, I was sure, 'Drum Screen Pit B was where I found Don. Could there be any connection?'

David said, 'That has to be a question for the police. But it's food for thought, isn't it?'

Peter said jerkily, 'If it wasn't Steve because he was in hospital, then how could it be Don who's been dead—'

'As I said just now,' David interrupted, 'it's a question for the police. We'll leave it for them, shall we?'

Peter looked as though he was going to say something else, but fortunately, at that moment, David's phone rang.

'Rossily . . . Oh yes, tell them I'll be with them directly. NII have arrived,' he said to us as he put the phone down.

'So this is it,' John said.

'Yes. You'd better get back to your departments. And please, try to give an impression of normality when they come round.'

We all started to get up.

'Not you, Michael.'

As the door shut behind us, I said, 'David, I'm sorry I was late—'

He waved me silent. 'It's not that. Were you out with Ms Brierly last night?'

'Yes. How did you know?'

'I guessed, by the way you couldn't wait to be gone at five. Enjoy yourself?'

'As a matter of fact, I did. Thank you.'

'Are you seeing her again?' Catching my expression, he said, 'Sorry, but I need to know.'

'Why?'

'You suggested yourself just now that Don's death might be part of what's going on. And there *is* something going on, isn't there?'

'Looks like it. But it doesn't involve Sarah.'

'How can you be sure?'

I told him what had happened when I'd quizzed her. 'I'm quite certain that she neither leaked the news about Don, nor knew anything about Steve.'

'But she did know that the story was going to be printed?'

'Her exact words were, "I'd been warned that something might be coming out."'

'Hmm. Are you seeing her again?'

'I don't know,' I answered truthfully.

'Try to, if you can.'

'Why?'

Pause. 'You do care about this station, don't you?'

'Of course I do. You know that.'

'If we get any more incidents like today, we could be

shut down. And that's something that would stick to us for years.'

'I agree,' I said with a shrug.

He said, feeling his way, 'I want you to stay close to Ms Brierly—not because she's necessarily involved,' he inserted quickly, 'but to pick up any information you can, meet the other organizers . . .'

'Mike Hempstead, secret agent,' I said ironically.

'Yeah. Why not?'

'Because, apart from anything else, I don't think she intends seeing me again.'

'Can't you tell her you've seen the light? They'd love a convert like you.'

'It wouldn't work,' I said impatiently.

'Why not—?' The telephone rang again and he snatched it up. 'Rossily . . . *Jesus Christ!*' he screeched into it. 'No comment, got that? No bloody comment.' He slammed the phone down. 'The *Western Evening* bloody *News* . . .'

'That might have been a mistake, David.'

He took a deep breath. 'Yeah. It might, mightn't it. I'll ring them back in a minute.'

'Why don't you organize a press conference?'

He looked up. 'That might not be a bad idea, you know. After we've heard what NII have got to say.'

He was phoning the *Western Evening News* to tell them he'd have something for them later as I left.

Back in my own office, I sat down and thought.

It didn't seem impossible to me that some of the wilder members of WANT might have the philosophy: *We know we're right, so where's the harm in giving the argument a helpful shove?*

The problem was the material they'd used to contaminate the sea-water, how could they have got hold of it? How did they get it into the system?

Was Peter involved? Was that why David had leaned on him so hard? Because he *had* leaned on him.

And where did Don fit in?

CHAPTER 12

NII didn't close us down, so David's call for normality must have worked. I thought I turned in an especially normal performance when they questioned me, 'they' being two men and a dried-up stick of a woman called Miss Underwood. It was she, however, who asked the most penetrating and informed questions. David and Sir hovered nervously around them.

Had I noticed anything out of the ordinary? they wanted to know.

No, I hadn't.

No anomalous readings on any chart recordings?

None.

Could I produce the charts?

Certainly.

Yes, very good. Did I have any idea of how the contamination could have arisen?

Hesitation . . . No. Given the data available to us, and the way the plant was functioning now, I couldn't think that there was any way it could be due to a fault in the plant.

Thank you, Mr Hempstead.

David came round to my office, grinning, just before twelve.

'We're off the hook, then?' I said.

'Yeah. They've told us to overhaul our security, but other than that, we're in the clear.'

'So they put it down to sabotage?'

'Mischievousness, to use their own word, but yes. And we've got a press conference arranged for this afternoon.'

'Today? How did you manage that?'

'It was Sir's idea. We're aiming it at the local press, but issuing a statement for any of the nationals that might be interested.'

'And are all the locals coming?'

'Pretty well.'

'Including the *Western Evening News*?'

'Especially the *Western Evening News*.'

I usually lunched in the canteen (quality variable, but cheap) but I drove home that day to think about things away from the station, I told myself. But as I admitted to myself in the car, it was the chance of seeing, maybe even talking to, Sarah.

She was there and she saw me. I was about to raise a pseudo-laconic hand and roar away when she called out, 'Michael, wait,' and ran over.

I drew in to the side.

'Michael,' she said breathily as she reached me, 'I was just wondering how I could contact you.'

She was wearing shorts and a cotton top.

'D'you want to get in a moment?'

'No, this won't take a moment. Liz—Elizabeth Tregenna, my boss—is having a few people to supper tonight. I thought you might like to come.'

David's words came back to me.

'I'd love to, but are you sure I'd be welcome? Does she know I work here?'

'Of course she does.' She smiled. 'And yes, you'd be more than welcome, they'll be falling over each other trying to convert you.'

'Ah, but is this gent for converting?'

She grinned shyly, slyly? 'I haven't given up on you yet.' Then, 'No, there won't be anything like that, I'd be surprised if Liz even mentioned nuclear power. You'll come, then?'

I nodded. 'Yes.'

'It's over at Dean's Lydeard. D'you know it?'

'Yes. D'you want a lift?'

'Please.' She smiled again. 'Although that's not the reason for asking you, either. Seven-thirty be all right?'

'Fine. I'll look forward to it.'

She straightened, took a pace back and I drove off thinking: Now you really have got something to think about.

Part of me was grinning, trying to ignore the other part.

Conversions. She and David had both mentioned them, but wasn't her own a bit sudden?

Unfortunately for David, the press conference didn't go quite as he'd hoped, although I only found out a little before five when he stalked into my office.

'Bastards! I'll have their guts for this. They're in league with those bloody women, they must be . . .' He pulled out his cigarettes and lit one, puffing furiously.

'Who are?'

'That's it! There must be a connection between them. If I can find it, prove it, I'll report them to the Press Council and then I'll—'

'David, suppose you stop sounding like King Lear for a moment and tell me what's happened.'

'Only the *Western* bloody *Evening News*, the bastards—'

'What did they do?'

'All the other papers, including one national, were reasonably civilized, but not the *Western Evening* bloody *News*, oh no—'

'David, what happened—?'

'*So now you've had a death from leukæmia, a murder and a radiation leak—*' a truly horrible falsetto voice—'*and all in the space of a week, yet you tell us everything's under control. And so on and so on.*' He drew heavily on his fag.

'Wasn't Sir able to put her down? I assume from your impersonation that it was a her?'

'One Katriona Litchfield, and a looker too. Or do I mean

hooker? No, Sir tried, but by that time, she'd got some of the others going too. If it hadn't been for her . . .' He mashed his cigarette in the side of my bin.

'Was sabotage mentioned at all?'

'Not as such, no. We'd decided beforehand not to, although I wonder now whether that was the right decision. No, we just said that NII had found nothing wrong with the station and given us a clean bill of health.'

'Not strictly true, so far as security goes.'

'We saw no reason to say anything about security.'

'It might not be as bad as you think, David.'

'I'm certainly not going to rely on that.' He took a breath. 'In fact, I've asked Doll to come over. He should be here soon.'

'But why? We can't prove sabotage.'

'No, but now that NII have found nothing wrong with us, there is a case to be answered. Besides, a third degree from the fuzz might just deter our female friends from any more girlish pranks.'

I said, 'D'you think Don's killing is connected?'

He hesitated. 'If it isn't, it's a hell of a coincidence.'

He asked me to stay and I was in his office with him when Doll arrived half an hour later.

'We've had the detailed PM on Mr Waterford now,' he told us once he was settled. 'He was hit eight, possibly nine times over the head with a heavy cylindrical object, probably metal. Some of the blows were a good deal heavier than others, suggesting a struggle. No metal fragments were found, suggesting stainless steel, or possibly chromium plate. He was dead before he hit the water.'

'No chance that it was an accident, then?' said David.

'None whatsoever. We've also been able to pinpoint the time of death more accurately, through examination of the stomach contents. We've discovered that he bought a meal from Lee's Chinese takeaway at approximately seven-fifteen. The state of the meal suggests that he was killed between eight and nine o'clock. He was then deposited in the Drum Screen Pit.'

'That is rather odd, now I think about it,' I said.

Doll raised his eyebrows at me.

'Well, whoever did it need only have taken the body a little further and dropped it into the Seal Pit and it would have been washed out to sea.'

Doll nodded sagely. 'A good point, sir, one that's already occurred to me. Suggests he might have been disturbed, by a security guard, perhaps.'

'I take it you've spoken to Security,' I said.

'I have. None of them noticed anything, but that doesn't mean our villain didn't notice them.'

'There is another possibility,' said David slowly. 'What if the body were meant to be found there?'

'What purpose would that serve, sir?'

'To embarrass us.'

'It would seem a rather extreme form of embarrassment, sir.'

'No, you're missing my point. It's why I asked you to come here. As you know, we've been picketed for some weeks by WANT, and now things have started happening. As I told you over the phone, in addition to the attempted sabotage of yesterday afternoon, we were successfully sabotaged last night. I'm suggesting that three of these events are connected; WANT, the murder and last night's sabotage.'

Doll paused before replying. 'That's an interesting theory, sir. Can you prove sabotage?'

'Not positively, no. But you can take it from me that that's what it was. Sabotage.'

Another pause. 'Can you suggest what the connection might be, sir?'

'Yes. The radioactive material that was used to contaminate the cooling water must have been smuggled out of the station somehow.' He leaned forward. 'Suppose Don

Waterford smuggled it out from the Cooling Ponds, gave it to the people behind this conspiracy, who then killed him, perhaps to silence him, and dumped the body, to embarrass us.'

Doll regarded him in silence for a while before saying, 'What has brought you to this conclusion, sir?'

'I've been thinking about it and it seems to me that Don had the best opportunity to acquire the radioactive material, since he worked closely with Peter Broomfield.'

'But wouldn't he, Broomfield, have had an equally good opportunity, sir?'

'Yes, but knowing the characters of the two men, I think Don the more likely, by a long way.'

Doll turned to me. 'Would you have thought Mr Waterford capable of this, Mr Hempstead?'

I hesitated. 'Put it this way. I certainly wouldn't have thought him *in*capable. There's something else that doesn't fit, though.'

They both looked at me.

'Don Waterford, or someone, might have smuggled some radioactive material from the Cooling Ponds, but surely he'd have then dropped it straight into the Drum Screen Pit rather than give it to someone outside, who'd then have to find a way of breaking in again.'

'And Waterford was dead long before the contamination took place,' put in Doll.

'Yes, yes,' said David impatiently, 'but he wouldn't have wanted the contamination to take place when he was anywhere near the station, would he? He'd have wanted an alibi. And the ladies outside might have wanted to contaminate the system at a time of their own choosing, to fit in with publicity, perhaps.'

'But how would they do it?' I asked.

'I don't know. Perhaps John was right and they did go out to the rig and drop the material into the intake grille.'

'But in that case, who killed Don?'

'All right,' David muttered. 'Just an idea.'

'No, you might be on to something, sir,' said Doll. 'Could Waterford have brought anyone into the station with him, who could then have killed him?'

'He could, but they'd have to be logged in with Security.'

'We'll check. Would it be possible for an outsider to break in on their own?'

'Security will tell you no, since they control the gates and an alarm goes off if anyone interferes with the perimeter fence. But someone who was really determined . . . ?' He shrugged.

'Hmm. Obviously, I need to have a further talk with Mr Broomfield at some stage. However, now I'm here, I'd like to go over some of the ground again, with your assistance. First, I have a list—' he extracted it from his folder—'of all the people who, according to Security, were in the station that night. Would you both look through it and tell me whether there is anyone who had any kind of special relationship with Waterford, good or bad?'

There were nearly fifty names on the list, headed by Sir, followed by David himself, then Rhiannon and John Burton. (They seem to be spending an awful lot of time together, I thought.) The others were nearly all shift workers of various grades and none of them had any special connection with Don that I was aware of.

There then followed one of the most frustrating hours of my life; when Doll said he wanted to go over the ground, he meant it literally.

First, we went to Security who told us that Don hadn't brought in any visitors recently, and that (as David had predicted) it was most unlikely that an outsider could break into the station without them knowing.

We then followed the route from where Don had worked in the Reactor Building to the Drum Screen Pits, from there to the Seal Pit, then from the station entrances to the Drum Screen Pits, and so on, while Doll measured distances, made notes and asked endless questions. After an hour, even David was visibly regretting having asked him to come in.

At seven, I told them firmly that, sorry, but I had to go. Doll wanted to keep me longer, but David, perhaps guessing where I was going, said that there was nothing I knew that he didn't. I left quickly before Doll could change his mind.

CHAPTER 13

It was nearly seven-thirty by the time I got home. I rang the Queen's Head with a message I'd be late, then showered and changed. The car needed petrol of course, but I decided to make a detour after I'd picked her up.

The journey from my house to the Queen's Head usually takes about five minutes. That evening, it took fifteen, thanks to some farmer who decided to move his sheep just at that moment. For some reason, being on a road seems to fill a sheep with an irrepressible urge to empty both bladder and bowels, so for ten minutes, I crawled behind this seething, bleating, stinking sea of woolly backs, trying to ward off the flies and getting hotter . . .

There was no sign of her when I arrived and I was at a loss to know what to do when the receptionist pointed to the bar. Which is where she was, on a bar stool sipping a long drink and looking a cool million dollars.

'I'm sorry I'm late, and I still need to get some petrol,' I said.

'Calm down,' she said, smiling. 'It's not the end of the world.'

'I *am* calm. Shall we go?' I said, conscious of the barman listening in.

'OK.' She finished her drink and slid off the bar stool.

She really did look good. She was wearing one of those short skirts that, being gathered, accentuate a woman's legs, making them look as though they go on for ever.

We went outside.

'Will we have to go much out of our way?' she asked, one foot in the car, the other still on the ground. 'For the petrol?' She smiled, knowing that I'd been looking at her legs.

'Not all that much.'

I was irritated, with myself for being so vulnerable, with her for making it so obvious. I started the car and swung it into the road.

'Lovely evening, isn't it?' she said.

'Yes, isn't it.'

She sensed my irritation and didn't say any more for a while. I bought some petrol, then took the road winding up through the trees to the top of the Quantocks. She looked around, enjoying herself again.

'It *is* a lovely evening,' she said. 'Isn't it?'

I nodded, smiling back at her. The low sun flickered in the trees, showering us with red and gold sparks.

We climbed higher.

'What are these trees?' she asked.

'Scrub oak. It's the wind and the altitude that makes them grow like that.'

'Weird,' she said. 'Creepy.'

I suppose they were, their thin, lichen-mottled trunks twisting round on themselves to make an almost impenetrable barrier. I know, having tried. Then these petered out, leaving just the heather and bracken and a few Scots pine.

'Good Lord!' She was looking over her shoulder. 'Stop a minute, Michael.'

I drew off the road beside a huge cedar whose lower branches touched the ground.

'Beautiful,' she breathed into the silence left by the engine.

The red sun, almost blood red, touched the surface of the sea, magnified by the heavy evening air.

'Yes.' I'd seen it before, but it *was* beautiful.

She twisted round to me. 'Why don't you say it as though you mean it?'

I leaned forward, touching her lips with my own. She returned the kiss for a moment before drawing back, laughing.

'That wasn't what I meant and you know it . . . Come on, let's go.'

Somehow, the contact had released some of the pressure inside me and we drove on in a companionable near-silence.

Lydeard's a large, rather straggling village with a lot of new estates, although the centre is still mostly original. It was there that we drew up, beside a largish cottage of old brick and roses. I zipped up the car and followed her up a cobbled path and under a trellis to a split door, the top half of which was open. To one side was a lean-to shed containing gardening tools and a couple of venerable bicycles.

'Hullo,' Sarah called out, tapping with the horseshoe knocker. I could see over her shoulder into a stone-flagged kitchen with a large old-fashioned table and a Welsh dresser. There was an answering call and footsteps, then a tall woman in a Laura Ashley dress strode across the room towards us.

'Sarah, darling.'

They embraced briefly, each kissing the air beside the other's cheek before turning to me.

'Liz, this is Michael Hempstead, the engineer at Desolation Point I was telling you about. Michael, Elizabeth Tregenna, chairperson of WANT.'

'How d'you do?' I said, taking the proffered hand. It was cool and dry and surprisingly strong.

'Hullo,' she said. 'Won't you both come through?'

Her eyes were a deep brown. She wore no make-up and her dark, almost black hair was threaded with a few that were white. Her profile as she turned revealed a strong, almost thrusting nose, but this didn't mar her severe beauty, or her femininity. I put her at about forty.

We followed her down a passage, also stone-flagged, to a large comfortable living-room, in which there were three other people, two men and a woman.

Elizabeth said, 'This is Michael Hempstead everyone, Sarah's friend.' She turned back to me. 'I'm sure you'll work out for yourself who's who, but I'll tell you anyway. Anna Linden, secretary of WANT.' She indicated a pertly attractive woman of about thirty with short blonde hair and blue eyes. 'And her husband, Tony.' A compact, good-looking man with an engaging grin, who at about five and a half feet, was little taller than his wife. 'And this is my husband, Jonathan.' This last was a tall, thin man with a full beard and a very sincere expression who stepped forward and solemnly shook my hand.

'We'll be eating soon,' continued Liz with a look at the grandfather (or should that be grandparent?) clock in the corner, 'but there's time for you to have an apéritif or a glass of wine first.'

Jonathan Tregenna poured us some white wine. He said, 'I believe you live locally, Michael.'

'Yes. On the other side of the Quantocks.'

'Ah yes, the Quantock Hills. They're out of this world, aren't they?'

'Yes,' I replied, 'they are.' Sarah slipped away to talk to Liz and the Lindens. I said, 'You've moved here quite recently, I take it?'

'Why, is that what all newcomers say?'

'Let's say the locals tend to take the countryside for granted. Where did you move from?'

He hesitated. 'We haven't moved, as such. I'm still based in London.'

'Oh, so this is a second home?'

'That's right,' he said, a trifle shortly. Then, 'I believe you're an engineer at the power station?'

'That's right,' I replied cheerfully.

'D'you find it interesting?'

'It has its moments. Mostly it's like most jobs, a day-to-day routine.'

'Forgive me, but I wouldn't have thought it possible to regard a job like that as routine.' He smiled, showing strong, very white teeth. 'I'd have thought you'd have been in a constant state of readiness to deal with an emergency.'

Here we go, I thought, a little surprised at the unsubtlety.

'If we were,' I said, smiling back, 'we'd all be nervous wrecks inside a month. And that *would* be dangerous. Besides,' I went on quickly, 'I don't think we've ever had a real emergency.'

'Oh?' His brow furrowed, lifting his eyebrows. 'I'd rather assumed that a radiation leak might come under the heading of real emergency.'

I smiled again. 'So it would, but we're happy now that there was no radiation leak as such. The Nuclear Installations Inspectorate visited the station today and gave us the all-clear.'

'But the radiation must have come from somewhere.'

'Indeed it must,' I said, watching him. 'The police are tending to the theory of sabotage.'

'Really? There was no mention of that on the news tonight. Sure you aren't indulging in a little wishful thinking?'

I said carefully, 'The police have noted the coincidence that this leak, the first we've ever had, should occur just as we're being . . . subjected to adverse publicity.'

'As you say, a coincidence. Although there are those who

might wonder whether previous leaks have gone undetected, or unreported.'

I took a breath. Was there any point in pushing this any further? No.

'Jonathan, I think we might end up bad friends if we pursue this topic.'

He gave a rather charming smile. 'I think you might be right. Forgive me for being such a poor host. More wine?'

'Thanks. Tell me,' I said as he refilled my glass, 'your name, Tregenna. Is it Cornish?'

'Yes, it is.'

'Are you from a long line of Cornishmen?'

'No, I'm not. Elizabeth is.'

I glanced over to where she was talking to Sarah and the Lindens.

'Well, I must say, she does look more Cornish than you. If you don't mind my saying so.' As I spoke, Liz left the room.

'Not at all. As you observed just now, it is a very old Cornish name, so when we married, we decided to take it instead of mine.'

'Interesting. To keep it going?'

Again he hesitated. 'Something like that.'

There was a slight pause. I said, 'What do you do for a living, Jonathan? If you don't mind my asking.'

'No, I don't mind. I'm a stockbroker, believe it or not.'

'It wouldn't have been my first guess,' I said slowly.

'No. Tony looks more the part than I do.'

'Yes, he does. So now I suppose you're going to tell me he's a Roman Catholic priest.'

He gave a polite laugh. 'No, he's a stockbroker too. We work in the same firm, my father's, as a matter of fact. But he's a better broker than I.'

'Ye-es,' I said. Then: 'I beg your pardon, I didn't mean to sound rude. But as you said yourself, he does look the part.'

At this moment, Liz came back into the room. 'If you'd all like to come through, supper's ready.'

As I followed Sarah down the passage, I thought about what Jonathan Tregenna had unwittingly told me about himself . . . pressed into joining the family firm and lacking the will to resist, now working with people better at the job than he, was it really surprising that he had married a woman like Elizabeth? I wondered what Sarah would make of my foray into psychology . . .

In the kitchen, Liz was saying, 'And if you'd like to sit here Tony, with Michael next to you . . .'

'What is this, Liz?' asked Tony good-naturedly. 'Boys on the left, girls on the right?'

'Something like that,' agreed Liz. 'Sarah, you sit here next to me, and Anna, next to Sarah.'

Tony and I were opposite Anna and Sarah, while Liz and Jonathan were at the ends of the table, Liz with her back to the door.

'Perhaps you'd all like to help yourselves,' she said.

This was followed by a good-humoured passing of dishes while Liz went round with the wine.

The main dish was a concoction of what seemed to be rice, aubergines and nuts held together with a sauce, and I suddenly realized there was no meat of any kind on the table. The other dishes held a potato salad, sweetcorn and mange-tout peas.

'Wine, Michael?' Liz was beside me. 'This one's rather nice, similar to what you were drinking before, but non-alcoholic.'

'If it's all the same with you, Liz, I'll stick with the first one. I rather liked it.'

'But aren't you driving?' The smile remained in place.

'Yes, but I don't think another glass of wine is going to hurt, do you?'

'Well, that's up to you, of course,' she said lightly, pouring me some.

'Thank you,' I said and took an appreciative sip.

'Nut pie, Michael?' This was Tony, proffering me the dish. A twinkle in his eye told me he'd taken in the brief clash.

'Thanks.' I took a couple of spoonfuls and then some vegetables from the other dishes.

We began to eat. To my surprise, the 'nut pie' wasn't just edible, it was delicious, perfectly set off by the vegetables.

'You live locally, Michael?' asked Tony, echoing Jonathan, who was talking to Anna, while Liz talked with Sarah. 'By the way, is it Michael or Mike?'

'Michael. And yes, I live in a village called Woodford on the other side of the Quantocks.'

'On the coast?'

'No, it's about two miles or so inland.'

'Don't let him get you on the subject of the sea or boats,' said Jonathan. I hadn't realized he'd been listening. 'He'll have you talking all night.'

A flicker of annoyance crossed Tony's face.

I said, 'That's all right, I'm interested in boats myself. You have a boat, Tony?'

'Yes, a small cruiser.'

'Oh, come on, Tony, it's a gin palace.'

'What utter rot, Jonathan.' Tony couldn't keep the irritation out of his voice.

'Where do you keep her?' I asked.

'St Katherine's Dock, at the moment.'

'Handy for London, but expensive, I should imagine.'

'Hellishly. The trouble is, if we kept her on the coast— Harwich, say—then we'd have to find the time to drive out there.' He addressed his remarks solely to me, effectively freezing Jonathan out of the conversation, and I wondered whether his irritation had its origins in a general resentment on Jonathan's part. Anyway, Jonathan took the hint and resumed talking to Anna.

Tony said, 'You have a boat yourself?'

'Yes, but it's only a dinghy. Not even a gin dinghy.'

He smiled reluctantly. 'Where do you keep her? The tides round here are pretty savage, I believe.'

'Watchport. D'you know it?'

'I've heard of it.'

We continued chatting in a companionable way. Liz was doing another round with the wine (I didn't argue with her this time) when a shadow darkened the upper half of the door and a voice called, 'Hullo, everyone,' and I looked up to see a strikingly good-looking girl with tumbled red hair.

'Cat!' cried Liz, moving quickly to the door.

I tried not to stare as 'Cat' said, 'Just thought I'd show my face as I was passing.'

Liz said, 'I'm glad you did, Cat. I wanted a word with you.' She undid the bottom door. 'Jonathan, be a dear and serve the pudding, will you?' She slipped out.

''Bye, everyone,' called Cat as she disappeared.

As Anna gathered the dinner plates and Jonathan went over to the fridge, I did some quick thinking.

'Cat', whom Liz didn't want to invite inside. Could she be any relation to Katriona Litchfield of the *Western Evening News*?

CHAPTER 14

'Enjoy your meal?' Sarah.

'Mm? Oh yes, very much, thanks.'

'More than you expected to, I'll bet.'

I grinned back at her. 'I'll not deny it.'

'Liz excels at this sort of thing. She trained as a food scientist.'

'Really? Does she do it professionally?'

'She did, before she married Jonathan.'

At this moment the food scientist came back in. 'How are you doing, Jonathan?'

'I can't find it,' he said in an undertone.

'It's in the fridge, didn't you look?'

'Of course I looked in the fridge.'

'It's all right, I'll take over now. Perhaps you'd put the bowls out.'

I watched her as she reached into the bottom of the fridge, took out a large basin and bought it to the table.

'Raspberry Pavlovina,' she announced. 'Like Pavlova, but with Greek yoghurt instead of cream.'

I've always disliked Pavlovas; the meringue's too sweet and the cream too sickly, but like the main meal, this was delicious. The sweetness of the meringue was perfectly offset by the sharpness and sourness of fruit and yoghurt. I told her so.

'Thank you,' she said. 'And I haven't thanked you yet for the trouble you took showing Sarah round your station. Especially considering the nature of our group.'

Thinking how nice it was of her to thank me so nicely for something I hadn't done for her, I said, 'I enjoyed it.' Well, some of it. 'It's our policy to be as open as we can with everyone.'

'Yes.' She paused. 'Since you're here, Michael, I was hoping that you wouldn't mind if we were to ask you one or two questions about your work. Try out some ideas on you. In your professional capacity.'

'No,' I said, knowing I couldn't refuse. 'I don't mind.' The truth was, I was surprised she'd chosen to bring it up like this, especially after what Sarah had said to me. I'd thought her the type who'd regard it as *de rigueur* to keep away from the subject.

'Jonathan darling, would you be an angel and make us some coffee?' She looked round. 'I take it we'd all like coffee?'

Heads were nodded around the table. Sarah rose and

collected the pudding bowls and took them over to the sink.

Liz said, 'Sarah was telling us after her visit how Somerset Nuclear Electric has a good deal of equipment in common with coal- and gas-fired stations.'

'That's true to an extent,' I said. 'The turbines, generators and condensing systems are all much the same.'

'The reason I'm asking this question is that we in WANT, unlike some of our friends in the Green Party, accept the need for energy generation—' she looked round for agreement—'and we'd hate to see all the effort put into building the station go to waste. Would it not be feasible to convert it to coal or gas firing?'

'I'd need to think about that,' I said slowly. What I was actually thinking was that maybe *de rigueur* had nothing to do with it, maybe this was Liz's way of taking my mind off 'Cat'.

'I'd have thought it a simple enough proposition.'

'In theory, yes, but there'd be several problems,' I said, overriding her. 'Firstly, nuclear power stations are sealed up after their useful life is over. I don't think it would be possible to bring in all the plant necessary for coal firing on top of that.'

'That's what we were afraid of,' said Anna.

'Another problem would be that you'd have to build a railway to bring in the coal.'

'That wouldn't be so difficult, would it?' Liz.

'Possibly not . . . it would be expensive, though, as would the transport costs afterwards. But the main thing that people don't seem to be able to grasp is that a coal-fired station emits many more pollutants, including radioactivity, than a nuclear-powered one.'

There was a chorus of protest.

'But nothing like so potentially damaging, surely?' Anna said.

'I wonder if the Germans who live near the Black Forest would agree with that, since half the trees there have been killed by the effects of acid rain from the coal-fired stations in this country.'

'But surely—' Liz, her enigmatic smile still irritatingly in place—'those emissions can be easily screened out at source.'

'Fitting out the existing coal stations would cost somewhere between a quarter and half a billion pounds each. Maybe a bit less when building a new station. You'd also lose a lot of efficiency.'

'A comparatively small price to pay on both accounts. I'd think.'

'Another thing to remember,' I ploughed on, 'is that coal is a finite resource.'

'But we've got two or three hundred years' worth of coal in this country alone, haven't we?' Anna.

'Yes, if you count total coal deposits, used at the present rate. But some of it's not going to be so easy to mine. Besides—' I raised my voice slightly to ward off interruptions—'a typical coal-burning station also releases, as its contribution to global warming, something like ten million tonnes of carbon dioxide a year, and that's not so easy to screen out.'

'So what do you think we should do, Michael?' Liz again. 'Close down the coal mines and put thousands of miners out of work?'

'No, Liz, of course not. British coal mines are the most efficient in Europe and coal should go on playing the major part in our power industry.'

'What about natural gas?' said Jonathan suddenly from behind me. 'It's available, efficient, easy to pipe, and I believe I'm right in saying that there are virtually no pollutants from a gas-fired station.'

'Well,' I said, turning round to face him, 'they emit carbon dioxide, and a lot of it. And if coal's a finite resource, natural gas certainly is; there's only about fifteen years' worth left in the North Sea. It seems to me an—'

'Oh, come. Reserves are always underestimated—look at North Sea oil.'

'But North Sea oil's running out, Jonathan. It seems to me an act of unbelievable crassness to waste such a versatile resource as natural gas by burning it in power stations.'

'If we substituted gas for nuclear,' he said, resuming his seat and leaning towards me, 'it would give us the necessary breathing space to screen the coal stations properly, and develop the renewable resources—wave and tidal power, solar and wind power.'

'Ah yes, the renewable resources. As I was telling Sarah only yesterday, tidal barrages are incredibly expensive to build, fifteen billion for one across the Severn. And as for wind power—if you covered the Somerset Nuclear Electric site with the latest type of wind generators, you'd still be lucky to get a hundredth of the power. When the wind blew, that is.'

'So you're saying that these renewable options shouldn't even be tried?'

'No, I'm not saying that, I'm saying—'

'Because it seems to me that you people want to keep them out just to protect your jobs.'

'I was asked for my views, Jonathan. The least you could do would be to listen.'

That earned me a silence.

'You talk about renewable energy—nuclear power is renewable, since nearly all the fuel can be reprocessed. It is safe, there have been no serious leaks, no one has died from radiation, our casualty record is virtually spotless compared with the coal industry—'

'How can you sit there and say that after Chernobyl?' demanded Jonathan. 'The same thing could happen here at any time. What you are doing is morally obscene.'

'It's a curious thing,' I said, 'but up until recently, I thought I was doing a worthwhile, useful job, generating the country's electricity. Now, I've suddenly become morally obscene.'

'Yes, I'm afraid you—'

Sarah said suddenly, 'Look, I'm sorry, but this isn't on. It's getting emotive, personal, and Michael *is* a guest, my guest—'

'Thank you, Sarah, I can look after my—'

'No, Sarah's quite right,' said Liz firmly. 'It has become emotive. Perhaps that was inevitable, given the nature of the subject, but we do owe you an apology, Michael. I'm sorry.'

'That's all right,' I said as easily as I could. 'I enjoy talking about my work.'

Liz continued, 'I suggest we forget about this and all go into the sitting-room now. Would anyone like a liqueur with their coffee?'

I had a brandy because I needed it. At least no one made any objection to that.

It was all very fine Liz saying: Let's forget what's been said and all be friends. Even though I could guess why it had been said, even though they now tried to draw me into the conversation, I still felt feather-ruffled and defensive.

I can't remember what they were talking about, but after a while Tony said quietly to me, 'If you don't mind my saying so, I thought you acquitted yourself rather well back there.'

'Of course I don't mind your saying so. I don't mind having to defend my views sometimes, but—' I lowered my voice—'it is so overpoweringly censorious here, isn't it?'

'You can say that again,' he said with a chuckle.

We were sitting a little way back from the others, after Jonathan had made a fuss about finding an ashtray for Tony (I noticed Sarah didn't have the moral courage to accept a cigarette from him), and now it was as though we had faded slightly into the background.

'I have to say, though,' he continued, 'that I agree with a lot of what they say about nuclear power. I just wish they weren't so . . .'

'Crusading?'

'Exactly. They do go over the top sometimes.'

'You said just now that you agreed with them. Have you always been anti-nuclear?'

'No, I was always fairly neutral about it until Chernobyl, but that made me think again.'

'As it did a good many people. It's certainly done the industry a lot of harm.'

At this point, we were 'spotted' by Anna and drawn back into the conversation, which actually wasn't such a bad thing. Anna had a bubbling sauciness to match Tony's acerbic wit, and now that we were all feeling a bit more mellow, their good humour was able to take over. It wasn't until a bit later I realized that leukæmia hadn't been mentioned in the 'discussion', and wondered whether it was because they were feeling guilty about the Holfords. At last Sarah said we ought to be going, so we said our goodbyes. Liz came out to see us off.

'It's been a pleasure,' she said when I thanked her for the evening, and she sounded as though she meant it. The 'discussion' might never have happened.

As soon as I'd driven off, Sarah put her hand on my arm.

'Michael, I'm truly sorry about what happened back there. It's not like Liz at all. I can't think what came over her.'

I can, I thought silently, wondering whether Sarah was being naïve or disingenuous.

'It didn't bother me all that much. Except for Jonathan. His—er—vehemence took me by surprise.'

'He was just defending Liz. He worships her.'

'Oh. Well, no real harm done. I rather liked Tony,' I added.

'Tony's all right,' she said after a pause. 'He's a bit of a smoothie, though.'

'I'll bet you're only saying that because he's a stock-broker. A successful one.'

'Maybe,' she said after another pause.

The night air was even more heady than before and we both gave ourselves over to it as the little car buzzed merrily up through the wooded hills. From nowhere, a hind appeared, her eyes glowing back at us before she disappeared weightlessly into the black of the trees. I felt Sarah start beside me.

Then we were on top of the hills, the Quantocks, stretching, interlocking in the muted moonlight . . . muted because the moon was a dusty, dusky red, a true harvest moon. Miles below, the sea carried the red scar of its reflection.

I pulled on to the verge beside the cedar tree where we'd stopped before.

'How unbelievably lovely,' Sarah breathed.

There was not a sound, just earth, sea and infinite moon. I don't know how long we stayed like that before my arm slid around her. She smiled at me . . . wryly? Regretfully?

She touched my hand where it lay on her shoulder, looked up again, asking to be kissed. I did, slowly at first, then greedily, until it felt as though we were consuming each other.

I drew back, touched her face, then her legs where they glowed in the moonlight.

She groaned, caught my hand, pressing it against her thigh. Then she released it.

Noises. The car door opening. My feet scratching the ground as I went round the bonnet to draw her out of the car, into the shadows beneath the tree.

Her legs were the most beautiful things I'd ever seen.

CHAPTER 15

She was in her usual place the next morning as I drove up and showed my pass to the guard. Our eyes met and a smile touched the corners of her mouth.

Oh, I admit it, I was on cloud eleven, so much so that when Rhiannon dropped into my office to ask about number three turbine, I was extra nice to her, a purely selfish, internal thing.

'You look shattered,' I said. 'Been burning the midnight diesel oil?'

'Mmm.' She nodded and smiled wanly. 'I wanted to get her up to Lydeard this weekend for tests. Doesn't look as though I'll make it now.'

'Problems?'

'You could say that.'

'Want to tell me?'

She looked at her watch. 'No, I'd better get on. Tell you later.'

I worked on autopilot, unaware of passing time until David phoned at around ten to ask me if I knew where Peter was.

'No,' I said. 'I didn't realize he wasn't in.'

'Well, he isn't. And I did check with him yesterday to make sure he would be.'

'Any reason why?'

He hesitated. 'Come on over and I'll tell you.'

But in his office, after inviting me to sit down, he didn't say anything, just stared at his desk.

'Well—?' I began, just as he said, 'I don't know quite how—'

I motioned for him to go on.

'Ostensibly, I wanted Peter in because of the improvements NII have told us to make in the Cooling Pond security. But that wasn't all.' He looked up at me. 'I take it you've noticed the state he's been in the last few days?'

'Well, it's obvious that Don's death has knocked him for six.'

'Yes, but should it have done? That much, I mean?'

'They were pretty good friends, and Peter's a lonely sort of bloke. And murder is murder.'

He breathed out. 'Yes, maybe you're right.'

'Well, come on. Now that I'm here, you might as well tell me what's bothering you.'

He looked up at me again. 'It'd crossed my mind that it might be guilty conscience.'

'Guilt about wh—' I felt my eyes widen. 'You don't think *he* killed Don do you?'

'No,' he said slowly, 'I don't think that. It had occurred to me, though, that if Don was involved in the sabotage, then Peter must have been as well.'

'Did Doll ever check his alibi for the night of the contamination?'

'I don't know. If he did, he didn't tell me.'

I stirred uneasily. 'You said guilt just now. You don't think he'd top himself or anything, do you?'

'No.' He shook his head impatiently. 'He likes himself too much, for all his self-imposed melancholy. I was thinking more along the lines that he might have done a runner.'

'You've never liked him, have you?'

'No,' he said carefully. 'That's one reason I wanted to talk to you about it first.'

'Have you tried phoning him?'

'Twice.'

'In that case, why not tell Doll about it? Get him to send someone round.'

He stood up and went over to the window. 'I'd rather not do that just yet.' He turned. 'I was going to suggest that we go round, and if he isn't there, check for signs of a hasty departure.'

I groaned. 'Why not just tell Doll and—'

'Because if I'm wrong, it wouldn't be fair on Peter.'

So I agreed to go. Sarah didn't notice me (probably wasn't expecting to see me in a Jag) but David noticed her and a spurt of gall crossed his eyes.

'Did you see her last night.'

'Yes.'

'Find out anything?'

'No, I didn't.' It came out without thinking.

Peter lived even closer to the station than I did, in the same village as Steve and Jane, so we were at his house within a few minutes. The first thing we saw there was his car.

'Which shortens the odds on a runner,' I observed.

David stopped his car behind Peter's and we walked to the front door. It was a mean little house, much worse than mine, and living in it can hardly have helped him after his divorce.

There was no bell. David brought the knocker down hard three times. Peered through the letter-box and shouted, 'Peter, it's me, David. We're worried about you. I don't like this,' he said to me, standing up.

I tried the door. Locked. Windows fastened and curtains drawn.

'The back,' said David.

But that was locked too, and the windows fastened. David looked around and picked up a garden spade. He was trembling.

'We ought to get Doll,' I said.

'No.' His voice trembled too. 'He might need help.'

'OK, but let me do it.'

Breaking glass always seems to make the most penetrating noise and I was sure someone must have heard and be ringing the police for us. I nicked my wrist opening the window (should have broken more of it), then had to clamber over a sink to get into the kitchen. There was a smell of whisky. I found the back door and let David in.

'Do we split up?' I asked.

'No.'

We found him in the first room we looked in, a sort of study. It was worse than I could ever have believed.

He was in a chair. I knew it was him because of the masklike face, masklike because there was very little of his head behind it. A double-barrelled shotgun lay between his knees. Something—thread? wire?—was attached to the triggers. The stench of stale whisky was overpowering and, incredibly, the dimness of the room was lit by the screen of his computer.

'Oh my God,' croaked David, and was sick on the floor behind me. I helped him out of the room. Sweat pricked my face and dizziness rang in my ears.

'Where's the phone?' I asked.

'Don't know.'

It was in the hall by the front door. I sat David on the stairs and reached for it.

'Fingerprints,' he managed, still croaking.

I found a handkerchief and dialled.

We waited in the car. We'd come out of the front because David couldn't bear to go past Peter again.

He'd cleaned himself up with a handkerchief. He was desperate for a drink of water but hadn't wanted to touch anything. He lit a cigarette and coughed over it. I got out of the car to look down the road.

The first police car arrived ten minutes later. I showed them where the body was.

Doll arrived fifteen minutes after that with the pathologist and took statements from us both. After this, he let us go because David said he had to inform NII and the Station Manager.

'Would you like me to drive?' I asked him when we got to the car.

'No, I'm all right now. I hope I never see anything like that again,' he added as we drove away. 'Ever.'

'NII won't close us down over this, will they?' I said a minute or so later.

'I don't think so, since it doesn't involve the safety of the plant. But they won't like it, on top of everything else. Hopefully, I can persuade them it's the logical conclusion to what's been going on here.'

'You accept that Peter killed himself, then?'

He glanced at me quickly. 'Yes. Don't you?'

'I suppose so, although I'd have agreed with what you said earlier, that he liked himself too much.'

'Well, it looks as though I was wrong, doesn't it? It could also be that you were right and he *did* kill Don.'

'But why?'

'I don't know. Maybe Peter wasn't involved in the sabotage, maybe he caught Don in the act stealing isotope, they fought, and . . .' By now we'd reached the gates. 'Whatever it was, I hold these bloody people responsible,' he grated.

'You think they somehow recruited Don?'

'I do, although it's for the police to find out.'

When we were back inside, he asked me to oversee Peter's work until he could organize something more permanent.

I felt a sense of complete unreality talking with the men, making decisions, knowing all the time that Peter was dead, but unable to acknowledge the fact. The men's jollity was indecent, but that wasn't their fault.

David and I had a late lunch together in the canteen, although neither of us ate very much.

'I've had Patricia on the phone,' he said in a low voice. Peter's ex-wife. 'She wants to come in and see me.'

'She's been told, then?'

'Yeah.'

'What about NII?'

'So far, it looks OK,' he said. 'They're not happy, obviously, but they say that as long as everything's covered, to carry on.'

'They didn't know about it already, then?'

'No, thank God. Although we can be sure of a lousy press when it does come out.' He looked up. 'Any chance you could make some inquiries along that line?'

'I'm seeing Sarah tonight,' I said. 'I'll see what I can do.' I paused. 'What does Katriona Litchfield look like?'

He drew in a breath. 'Tallish, five seven or eight. Attractive and knows it. Well-spoken in a Hooray Henrietta sort of way. Mass of red hair. Why?'

So it was definitely her. 'You've just asked me to make inquiries, haven't you?'

Doll turned up at about four. He spoke to us in David's office.

'First, I'd like you both to look over your statements.' He handed us typed copies, which we read and agreed were accurate.

'Good. Now I'd like to ask you both a few questions. To begin with, I'm still a little unclear as to why you went to Mr Broomfield's house in the first place.' He was looking at David.

He gave me a fleeting glance before replying. 'I was expecting Peter in today. When he didn't turn up, I phoned him, twice. When there was no answer, I began to worry and asked Michael here to accompany me to his—'

'Let me stop you there, sir. Is this something you do routinely if someone doesn't turn up for work?'

'Not routinely, no. But as I said in my statement, I've been worried about him ever since Don Waterford was killed.'

Doll didn't say anything, just looked at him, and after a moment he continued.

'They were friends, buddies. Peter had taken Don's death very badly and was in a morbid frame of mind.'

'Are you saying that you thought something of the kind might happen, sir?'

'No, I'm not saying that,' David replied with a touch of asperity. 'I was just worried.'

'I still don't understand why *you* had to go.'

'There wasn't anybody else.'

'What about Mr Hempstead here?'

'I felt there should be two of us.'

'Why was that, sir?'

'Because I felt uneasy, dammit! Haven't you ever felt uneasy?'

Doll ignored this and turned to me. 'Did you regard it as a reasonable thing to do, Mr Hempstead?'

'Certainly. I'd seen for myself how strange Peter's mood had been.'

David said, 'Is there something suspicious about Peter's death, Inspector? I mean, I don't understand this line of questioning.'

'If you could bear with me, sir.' He paused. 'The two men were friends. Suppose Waterford, as you suggested earlier, was in some sort of collusion with WANT, would he have told Broomfield about it?'

'I . . . don't know.' David came to a decision. 'The fact is, Inspector, we have been wondering about that . . .' And he told him how we'd wondered whether Peter had been involved in the contamination, or alternatively, whether he in fact had killed Don.

Doll thought about this. At last he said, 'Broomfield's alibi was solid for the night of the contamination, he was at his ex-wife's house, although he had no alibi for when Waterford was killed. But why would he have killed his closest friend?'

David shrugged. 'I don't know. It did occur to us that

he might have found Don trying to smuggle out isotope, or something.'

Doll studied him thoughtfully. David continued, 'Have you come to any conclusions yet? About how Peter died.'

'Early days yet, sir. However, what evidence we have so far does indicate suicide.'

'D'you know when it happened?' I asked.

'The pathologist thinks sometime between ten last night and two this morning, although we should have a more definite time later.'

'Didn't anybody hear anything?'

'No. Which is not altogether surprising, since the nearest house is about fifty yards away.'

'Still, a shotgun blast . . .'

'The cottage has thick walls. Also—' he hesitated—'the noise would have been muffled to an extent anyway. He put the barrels in his mouth.'

David stirred uneasily.

Doll continued, 'And the method he used, tying thread to the triggers and then to his toe. It's quite well known.'

'So you're happy—sorry, wrong word—satisfied, that it was suicide?'

'Early days, as I said, sir. But there is the fact that he was depressed. Also . . . I don't know whether either of you noticed the message on the computer screen?'

'I noticed it was on,' I said.

He took his notebook out.

'*No choice. First Pat, now Don. Why did he ever let them talk him into it? Pat, I'm so sorry,*' he read out.

'Is that exactly how it was written?' I asked.

'Yes, and the fact is, messages as bizarre as that tend to be authentic. As is, too, the fact that he didn't leave his name with it. So we now have to decide whether he did actually kill Waterford, and if so, why?'

'Does the message help?' I asked.

'It might. *First Pat*, his wife, whom he'd failed, or so he thought. *Now Don.* His friend, whom he'd killed? Then: *Why did they let him talk him into it?* This could mean that Waterford was in fact in league with WANT. There's no doubt it does hang together.'

After this, he got us to sign our statements, then made to leave.

As David handed his back, he said, 'You will keep us up to date, Inspector?'

'As far as is practicable, sir. Oh, there was one other thing. Perhaps, as a formality, you could both tell me where you were between ten last night and two this morning?'

David chuckled briefly. 'I was wondering when you'd get round to that. My wife and I visited friends in Bath last night. We didn't leave till gone midnight and were home sometime after one. I doubt if we were asleep much before two.'

'If I could have the name and address of your friends, sir?'

After he'd noted them, he turned to me.

'I was with a friend as well, until about midnight. I was home about twelve-thirty and went straight to bed. Alone,' I added, thinking of Sarah. I gave him her name and address, and those of the Lydeard crowd.

David saw him out, then turned back to me. 'So you were with her WANT friends last night?'

'Yes.'

'That was sneaky. Why the hell didn't you tell me about it earlier?'

'It was arranged at the last minute.' Then, becoming irritated, I continued, 'Also, in the final analysis, it's none of your business.'

He lit a cigarette, then said quite mildly, 'It is my business, sunshine. Those women are trying to sabotage *my* station—*your* station. They could also be morally responsible for two deaths. You'd better think about where your loyalties lie.' He drew on his cigarette. 'Are you that keen on her?'

'Yes, I'm keen on her.'

'Still sure she's not playing you for a sucker?'

'Yes, I am sure.'

But am I? I wondered as I went back to my own office. Is that why I'd lied? Because I have to know first for myself whether she's involved?

But something else was worrying me even more.

It had been something of a joke among the others that David, Peter and I all disliked diminutives. We were never Dave, Pete or Mike. But Peter had taken it a stage further in that he always referred to his wife as Patricia, never Pat, even although others did. And I was sure he never would, not even in a suicide note.

CHAPTER 16

I looked at the beautiful drowned face beside me and couldn't spoil it—not yet. I could see the down on her cheeks, the colouring of her skin. Her nose flared slightly as she breathed and a tiny pulse beat in her neck . . . She must have sensed me looking at her because her eyes opened and swivelled round to me. She smiled and reached out.

'Mmm. Come here.'

I was to have collected her from the Queen's Head, but she'd rung me just after I'd got home.

'I did something really stupid last night,' she'd said.

'Wouldn't necessarily agree with you there.'

She chuckled. 'No, not that. I left my bag with my keys in it at Liz's and had to knock the landlord up. It was so embarrassing.'

'Why didn't you give me a ring? You could have stayed here.'

'I would have, if I could have got to a phone. Anyway, he'd only just gone to bed, fortunately.'

'Have they given you another key?'

'Yes, but that's not why I rang. Anna and Tony are on their way back to London and have brought my bag back for me. They're going to drop me at your place.'

'Tell them not to bother, I'll pick you up.'

'Oh, don't be a spoilsport. I think Anna's a bit curious about where you live.'

'Oh, all right. So long as they don't stay too long.'

In the event, they'd stayed for a coffee and their company hadn't been at all tiresome.

'Whatever it was that you two young things were dashing away for last night must have been very important,' observed Tony, straight-faced. 'To cause Sarah to forget her handbag, I mean.'

'Oh, shut up, Tony,' said Sarah, her cheeks flushing faintly.

'Yes, you are the limit,' agreed his wife. Her eyes had been flicking around my living-room, so maybe Sarah had been right.

'So you're off back to London for the weekend?' I said.

'Yes. Seems a bit arse-about-face, doesn't it, but there you go.'

'Must you be so crude all the time?' demanded Anna.

'Sorry,' he said contritely. 'It's me genes. I can' 'elp it.'

We saw them off (in a rather nice black Porsche), then went back in. Sarah tut-tutted over the contents of my larder for a while before making a very creditable Spaghetti Bolognese.

'Maybe *you* should have been the food scientist,' I said.

She smiled land shook her head. 'No. I like what I do.'

'Being a Probation Officer, or protesting?'

'Both.'

When we'd eaten, we drifted up to bed.

After we'd slowly made love for the second time, I got up.

'Like a coffee?'

'Mmm.'

'I'll bring you one.'

But by the time I did, she was up and dressed herself, looking out of the window.

'Summer's nearly over, isn't it?' she said sadly as I put the mug on the sill behind her.

I glanced out. The sky was darkening, but that was because a bank of grey cloud was covering it from the east. I stepped back and sat on the bed.

She turned. 'Want to tell me about it?'

'How did you know there was an it?'

'Oh, there's obviously something on your mind. Glad I was able to make you forget for a while.'

'And some.'

She laughed and came to sit beside me. 'That's what I like about you, you're so appreciative. Makes me feel . . .'

'Like a woman?'

'Pig.' She jabbed me in the ribs. 'Come on, tell. Auntie Sarah's listening.'

'It'll spoil things.'

'You don't know that until you try me, do you?'

So I told her about the press conference and how angry David was with the *Western Evening News*.

'The "Cat" who popped in last night and popped out again so quickly was Katriona Litchfield, wasn't she?'

She pressed her lips together and nodded. 'When you didn't say anything last night, I thought she'd got away with it. Have you told your boss?'

'Not yet. I wanted to hear what you had to say.'

She took a breath and released it.

'She's an old friend of Liz's. I didn't like the idea, but

Liz thought it too good a chance to pass up. What with that, having the cottage in Dean's Lydeard and the Holford leukæmia case, she thought the gods were smiling on her so far as Desolation Point went.'

'Was it you who broke the story after we found Don's body?'

'No, I told you before, it wasn't.' Her clear grey eyes held mine. 'When I give my word, I keep it.'

I believed her.

But is that just because I want to believe her? I asked myself, remembering her apparent naïvety when we'd driven away from Liz's house.

'Forgive me?' she said now.

After a pause I said, 'I can probably forgive you that. But something much worse has happened.'

'What?' She looked genuinely puzzled.

Impulsively, feeling a little foolish, I took her hand.

'Please tell me the truth. Did Liz, or any of you, bribe any of the staff at the station to contaminate the cooling water?'

She pulled her hand away. 'Of course not! Apart from anything else, I wouldn't know how to go about bribing anyone, neither would any of the others. Anyway, there's no need for us to use tactics like that, not when your station really does leak radiation.'

'But it doesn't,' I said tiredly. 'It was sabotage, arranged, we think, by Don Waterford, the man we found in the Drum Screen Pit.'

She looked at me, shaking her head slightly. 'But that was nothing to do with us. Are you trying to suggest that we killed him?'

'I don't know what to think any more, it's all such a mess. Look, can I trust you not to repeat what I'm about to say?'

She hesitated, but curiosity overcame her.

'All right, yes. So long as it's not something that could

endanger the public. Can I have *your* word on that?'

'Yes.' And I told her about Peter.

She stared at me, her mouth open. 'But that's horrible! The poor man. You're not having me on, are you?'

I shook my head.

She closed her eyes a moment. 'OK, so you think this Peter killed Don and then himself. He must have been unbalanced, insane.' She opened them again, focused on to me. 'What if it's some sort of isotope you're using that drove him insane?'

I groaned. 'By now, we'd all be killing each other off. A lot of people have been there a lot longer than Peter.'

'But what if he were just more susceptible, like some people are with cancer?'

'The point is—listen—I don't think he did kill himself.' I told her why not.

This time, she really did look scared. 'Have you told the police?'

'No.'

'Why not?'

'I wanted to hear what you had to say. To hear the post-mortem result. I wanted to think about it.'

She thought for a moment herself, then, 'It is a bit thin, isn't it?'

'How so?'

'Well, who can tell what's going through the mind of a man who's about to kill himself? Perhaps, in his state of mind, he just called her Pat.'

I shook my head. 'It's not him. He just wouldn't.'

She continued staring at me. 'So who do you think did kill him?'

I shrugged. 'I've no idea.'

She said, her voice rising, 'Or are you trying to pin this one on us as well?'

At that moment the phone rang, which was perhaps fortuitous. I went downstairs and picked it up.

'Michael? It's Anna, Anna Linden.'

'Oh, hello, Anna.'

'Look, I know this is going to sound really stupid, but I think I've left my keys at your house.'

'Oh no. Are you locked out?'

'No. Luckily Tony had his, but I'd like to know where mine are.'

'Naturally.' My eyes cast around the living-room. 'I have to tell you that they don't exactly leap to view.'

'I did use your bathroom, remember. Look, Michael, would you be an angel, have a quick look round and ring me back?'

'Sure. Has Sarah got your number?'

'Yes, but I'd better give it to you anyway.'

I found a pencil and took it down. It was inner London, I noticed.

'Thanks, Michael,' she said. 'I really am grateful.' I heard her saying something to Tony as she put the phone down.

'Was that Anna?' Sarah asked from the stairs.

'Yes.' I told her what had happened. 'That'll teach them to do good deeds.'

We looked around but couldn't find any keys and I was on the point of calling Anna back to tell her so when the phone rang again.

This time it was Kenny Parrish from the station.

'Sorry to bother you, Michael, but the shift engineer's called me in again. The alarms on the condensers have gone off. They seen to be losing efficiency.'

'What are the readings?'

He repeated them to me. 'And that's after we've in-creased the flow of water.'

'Is this on both reactors?'

'Yes.'

'Does David know about it yet?'

'He's not answering his phone.'

'All right. I'll be with you in—' I looked at my watch
—'give me ten minutes.'

'Problems?' said Sarah from behind me.

'Yes. I've got to go into the station. If I'm not back in
an hour—'

'Yes?'

'Look, I don't know how long I'm going to be. Why don't
you stay the night?'

'I'm sorry, Michael, I can't, not tonight.'

'All right. I'd better run you back now.'

'Will you ring Anna while I get my things?'

She went upstairs while I did so and three minutes later
we were on our way.

'What is the problem?' she asked.

'The real problem is that they can't contact my boss.
Otherwise, it's just a routine irritation,' I lied. 'Can I see
you tomorrow?'

She took a while to reply and when she did, I could
hardly hear her.

'I'm not sure that we should go on seeing each other.'

I went cold. 'Sarah, we can't leave it like this.'

'I suppose not. Can I ring you tomorrow?'

We drew up at the inn. 'OK, but if you don't, I'll come
looking for you.'

She gave me a rather wan smile, a quick kiss and was
gone. I turned back to the station.

It's so different at night. By day, it's filled with life and
energy, and I don't mean the generators, I mean the energy
of a thousand people. At night, there are barely fifty.

Empty offices, corridors, workshops. The Turbine Hall
full of noise, empty noise among a thousand leagues of
pipework.

There was life at the perimeter, though: cooking fires,
torches, dimly lit tents. I showed my pass and hurried over
to the Control Room. Kenny met me at the door, a worried
expression on his face.

'No better?' I asked.

'It's getting worse.'

'Still no David?'

He shook his head and I followed him over to the instrument panels. The shift engineer moved so that I could read them. Temperatures weren't near Scram level yet, but they were certainly high, and rising. Water flow and vacuum were both down.

'Have you tried increasing the flow again?'

'No.'

'Well, let's give it a try now, shall we?' I turned the dials up a few notches.

No change.

Twisted them round to the stops.

Still no change, nothing. I turned them some way back to avoid overloading the motors.

Kenny said, 'I wonder if there's a blockage over the intake?'

'It could be that, from the readings.'

Decision time: do I go over David's head to Sir, and risk dropping him in it?

Back to the instrument panels—the readings seemed to have steadied. No, not until we were nearer Scram level. Not yet.

'Kenny, I think we've got half an hour. I'm going over to the rig to see if I can see anything down there on the new equipment. I'll phone you.'

'But what can you do about it if you do see anything?'

'I'll worry about that when I've had a look.'

I took the lift down and ran over to the seaward gate. A north-easterly breeze had risen, moving the branches of the tamarisks beyond the fence. I pushed in my card-key and went through.

Cloud covered most of the sky now, leaving just a thin band of light in the west which danced over the water, making it seem lighter than it really was.

The dinghy was floating on the high tide. I pulled the cover away, stowed the piece of timber that held it up and turned on the petrol. Then felt round for the lifejacket . . .

Oh, sod it!

I looked back at the steps in the sea wall. It would take at least ten minutes to find one. Sod it.

I pulled the cord and the engine started third time as it always did. I checked the oars and cast off. The screw bit encouragingly into the sea and I followed the buoys that marked the channel through the rocks. A little way out, the wind grew, slapping the waves against the hull.

I found the torch, tied up and gingerly climbed the iron steps to the platform. A quick glance round, then into the cabin where I switched on the sensors, gave the screen a few moments to warm up, then did a sweep.

Nothing. Much. I rang Kenny, who answered straight away.

'I can't see anything, just a vague lump floating around that might be seaweed. How're things at your end?'

'Temperatures've started rising again. Not fast, but if it keeps up, we're going to Scram before much longer.'

'We'll give it another five minutes. If they're still rising then, I'll ring Sir.'

I put the phone down and went back outside. The wind was getting up and waves slapped sullenly against the metalwork of the platform.

I glanced over to the station. It was like a village in the Middle East: waving tamarisks against pinpoints of light. The glass panels of the Reactor Building reflected the western glow, gleaming as though from the power within.

I shone the torch down on to the oily water. Nothing, just ridges, troughs and bubbles.

Back to the cabin.

There was certainly something down there . . . I adjusted the controls, trying to get a better picture. Then it suddenly occurred to me that whatever it was was indistinct because it was out of focus, at or near the same level as the sensors . . .

The phone rang.

'Hello.'

'It's Kenny. The temperatures are going up fast. I tried to increase the flow again, but it's no good. We'll Scram at any minute at this rate . . .'

'Both reactors?'

'Yes, I—'

'Phone Sir now. Tell him I'm on the rig and that I'll stay here until he tells me otherwise.'

Back to the instruments. What the hell was it?

Outside again. Torch beam on the oily water. Waves and bubbles . . .

You expect to see bubbles on the sea.

But this many?'

The wail of the klaxon jerked me up, then the PA system boomed over the water.

Attention, attention all staff, both reactors about to Scram, I repeat, both reactors about to—

The voice was cut off by the scream as, one by one, the safety valves lifted and expanding plumes of steam tore into the sky, glowing faintly in the light from the horizon.

I shone the torch on to the water again. Bubbles . . . ?

Although I couldn't have heard anything in the noise from the steam, something made me look round.

A nightmare figure dripping black. It took a swing at me with a bar, missed . . . I fell against the railings, turned, tried to jump into the water, but I was too late, too late . . .

CHAPTER 17

Waves slapping—no, caressing, plinking against the sides of the boat . . . why am I lying in the bottom, why am I so cold?

I raised my head, which was immediately smote a mighty blow—from within. I groaned, sank back and waited for it to pass. It didn't. Cautiously I felt my head and found a blood-encrusted bump—I'd been hit!

I pulled myself up, clinging to the seat. Couldn't see a thing. Tried taking deep breaths to clear my head.

Where was the station? I looked around slowly—fast movement hurt too much. Couldn't see anything.

A larger wave rocked the boat and I clung to the seat, shivering. I was cold to the bone.

A noise. I listened . . . Waves on a shore, and not far away.

Where the hell was it?

Another deep breath, look slowly around, try and concentrate on each field of vision.

A cluster of lights, a town, biggish, a long way off . . . Wales?

I blinked and peered again . . . Cardiff? Barry?

Slowly, I turned and peered into the opposite direction . . . nothing. Looked up, and saw the faintest glow where a cliff ended and the sky began.

I tried to think. Cliffs, yes, the tide would have taken me down channel, but how far? It had been high tide, so a good way. Ten miles? More?

I could hear the waves breaking over the shore more clearly now, clearly enough for me to realize it wasn't a shore. It was rocks, which was only to be expected along this stretch of coast.

I felt around feverishly—didn't even know which end of
the boat was which—found the bow, worked my way back
to the transom. No outboard. And no oars—although the
length of timber for propping the cover up was still there.

I sat up on the seat, shivering. The tide was probably
on the turn, the onshore wind blowing me on to the rocks
and there was nothing I could do about it.

What could I do? Try to fend the boat off? Jump out
and make for shore? Ha bloody ha! Fine chance on this
coast, especially without a lifejacket.

A grating noise as the boat scraped over something—it
slewed, nearly tipping me out and a wave slopped over the
side. Jesus! What was I going to do . . . ?

The boat righted. I panted, swallowed.

Then I saw light. The cloud had thinned and the moon
come out. I risked standing and could see that I was a
hundred, a hundred and fifty yards from the cliff, all of
them covered in weed-strewn rocks.

A wave drove the boat forward. I dropped to my knees,
grabbed the timber and thrust it at a rock—and the boat
heaved past.

At least I knew what I had to do now. Another rock,
push, drifted by. I looked ahead and saw a massive one,
about twenty yards away—but there seemed to be a passage through to the left of it . . .

I thrust the timber down into the water, found something, pushed . . . and again . . .

Then the light died.

Frantically I kept pushing, anything to get the boat over
to the left . . .

Another wave, the boat scraped something—*push*—then
I fell forward as it drove into the rock. A wave burst over
the side, half filling it, then we were scraping reluctantly
round the side.

The boat was heavy now, the bottom bumping against
every . . .

Another wave lifted it, pushed it forward. Then the moonlight came on again, only for a second or two, but enough to see the cliff about eighty yards ahead. If I could just keep going like this . . . but there was a biggish clump of rock coming up . . .

I thrust down with the timber, couldn't find a purchase, another wave lifted and carried the boat, I crouched, knowing we were going to hit . . .

This time we struck sideways on. I tried pushing but it wouldn't move, then a wave crashed over the side, filling the boat completely. I got up on the seat, thrust my hands forward into a mass of bladderwrack, no use trying to climb, I'd slip . . .

Then another wave lifted both the sunken boat and me and instinctively, I sprang. My foot slithered on the weed and I fell, tearing my hand on something, a limpet probably as the water surged over me . . .

I pushed myself up, peering into the darkness. Nothing for it, I had to go on. I crawled forward until I felt the rock slope away, then, waiting until the next wave had passed, brought my feet forward and lowered myself down, scraping over projections, limpets, God knows what . . .

My feet had just touched bottom when another wave took me and I had just time to throw my arms forward and fend off the next rock. The flow of water sucked me round it and at last, I felt my feet touch a shingle bottom.

Arms out-thrust, I managed five paces in the slack water before tripping, but a wave took me on, past more rocks . . . I got to my feet, four more paces against the undertow, water only up to my thighs now, then another wave threw me forward—straight into a big rock and it was only the fact that it was covered in bladderwrack that saved me from knocking myself out . . . round it, forward, water only up to my knees . . . nine, ten paces against the undertow . . .

The rocks were smaller now and I felt, crawled, clambered over them until at last I found a thin bank of coarse, dry shingle, where I lay on my back, heaving in air, staring at the blank sky above. I knew where I was.

Once I got my breath back, I began to think. Although most of the coast west of the station is rocky, it's still poss- ible to walk along nearly all of it—until you get to Northhead. The three or four miles below North Hill are so rocky as to make casual walking impossible, although in daylight you can go along very slowly by jumping from rock to rock. But not at night. And especially not in total darkness.

However, a lot of the cliff is climbable, once you get past the first ten or twenty feet. That tends to be composed of shale, a form of hard flaky clay that's said to contain oil. Whether it does or not, it's terrible stuff to climb, because it's slippery, and crumbles if you put any weight on it.

There was still a stiff onshore breeze and I'd begun to shiver again. I cautiously got up and made my way over to the cliff face. Shale. I began to work my way along, looking for a place to climb against the dim light in the sky.

The cliff is mostly concave at ground level where it's been scoured out by the spring tides, projecting at about head level or above, which is why those first ten or twenty feet are so difficult. Every now and then, there's a bit where there's been a landslide, or the end of a combe that can be climbed.

The shingle petered out and I was back to clambering over rocks again, slowing me down a lot. After about ten minutes, though, I found a suitable place; in fact it looked like the end of a combe, maybe even the one Sarah and I had walked down.

I began feeling my way over the rocks that led up into it. Soon, this gave way to coarse grass and heather, then the combe, if it ever had been one, disappeared, leaving me with just a fifty-degree slope. It was still fairly easy to climb, though, and I kept going. The gorse didn't start until about three hundred feet.

There wasn't much, and at first I hardly noticed it. Then it became thicker and I paused to get my breath back. The light was still very dim, but here, at three hundred feet, the sea seemed to glow faintly, making it easier to get bearings. I looked up. Only another seven hundred feet to go.

I started up. The gorse grew thicker, but I was able to weave my way through it and it didn't bother me. Much. I must have been at five hundred feet before it began seriously to slow me down.

I stopped, looked around. Couldn't see how far it extended in any direction. Might not last much longer. Keep going.

Fifty feet later, I wished I'd turned back. It had become so thick that each step up required a huge effort. My legs were trembling with the strain, not to mention the pain as the spines dug into my thighs and hips.

I could still go back down . . .

And lose three hundred feet, with no guarantee that there was a better way . . .

Keep going. I pushed forward a few more paces before stopping again.

What if I went down on all fours and tried crawling between the trunks?

I got down, but they were growing too close together . . .

As I pushed myself to my feet again, my head throbbed so madly I thought I was going to faint.

Deep breaths.

Stay still. Ignore the gorse spines, your trembling legs, the sweat running down your face—yes, sweat, when half an hour earlier I'd been shivering . . .

Nothing for it.

Take ten paces.

Rest. Breathe. Ignore the pain in your head.

Ten paces.

I don't know how long it took me to climb up through that gorse. Ten paces became five, three. I whimpered with the pain in my head, clean forgot the gorse spines, put all my concentration into keeping my legs moving. Knew that if I stopped for any length of time, I'd never get started again . . .

If I were to collapse and die, I thought, I'd never be found. Who would ever come here?

At last, incredibly, the gorse began to thin and be replaced by heather as the slope grew shallower. It was thick heather and often I tripped, but at least it absorbed the shock.

If I keep going, I thought, I must reach the road. Ground almost level now . . . how much longer? . . . and what the hell is that?

I stopped.

Something, ahead of me, was bounding through the heather, over it rather, two bounds a second . . . Shush-shush, shush-shush . . . straight towards me.

A sheep? No, too purposeful, deliberate.

A hare? Too big.

Dog?

It was coming nearer, maybe ten yards. I felt the hairs on the back of my neck rising.

I shouted at it—*Aarrh!*

It stopped.

I shouted again, jumping towards it . . .

It started moving again, not towards me, but in a circle around me . . . Shush-shush.

I turned to keep facing it, shouted again.

Deliberately, not hurrying, it kept moving around me, not uttering a sound. It stopped after a hundred and eighty degrees.

Not a sound.

I swallowed, jumped and shouted again, except that it came out as a croak.

Then, after a pause, it began moving away from me, on its previous course. Not hurrying.

I started walking again, trembling all over, stopping every few paces to listen.

Nothing.

Ten minutes later, I found the road.

CHAPTER 18

And about an hour after that, I walked, staggered, into Northhead. I'd fallen several times, once quite badly, cutting my elbow. I'd only kept going because it was all downhill and I was scared.

The town was deserted. A clock struck three. Hospital or police? Hospital—

'Good evening, sir.' A copper, and I hadn't even heard him. He looked at me closely. 'Been in a fight, have we, sir?' He pulled out his notebook. 'Perhaps if I could have your name?'

'Michael Hempstead . . .'

The lunacy of the night returned and I was back, corkscrewing down the road from North Hill, in the dinghy as it ran on to the rocks, standing in the heather as the thing circled me . . .

I sat up to find myself on a bed with a nurse holding my shoulders and saying, 'It's all right.' A doctor was binding my arm and behind them sat the policeman. As he saw me, he said, 'Don't worry, sir, I know who you are now.' Then he got up and walked purposefully away.

I thought: It's amazing how different the word *sir* can sound, contemptuous or respectful . . .

'How are you feeling?' asked the doctor, a young Asian with bags under his eyes.

'I'd give anything for a drink of water.'

The nurse fetched a glass and helped me drink it, and then another.

'Better?' asked the doctor.

'My head hurts like hell.'

'It would. That's a nasty crack you have on the back of it.'

I raised my hand and felt the bandage round it.

'Our friends the police will shortly be wishing to ask you some questions. Do you feel up to it?'

'I do not.'

'Very well then, they can wait until tomorrow.' He snipped away the ends of the bandage. 'The nurse will give you a sedative and get you into bed.'

I don't know what the sedative was, but it was marvellous. My head still hurt, but it didn't matter, I just sank into a beautiful oblivion.

The first person I saw when I woke was a nurse, not the same one. Sitting beside her was a WPC with a notebook.

'How are you feeling?' the nurse asked.

'Not sure. My head still hurts.' I moved my body experimentally. 'Jesus! I hurt all over!'

'You would,' the nurse said, laughing.

'Well, I'm glad you think it's funny.'

'It's not that, it was your expression. Also, it means that there isn't much wrong with you.'

'Thanks.' I gazed down at the tube sprouting from my arm. 'I'd always heard that nurses were tough little cookies underneath all the sweetness.'

'Propaganda put about by our enemies.' She got up. 'I'll get you something for your head, then the officer here wants to ask you some questions.'

I made a face and the nurse said to her, 'Please, only ten minutes.'

Actually, it didn't take long, the police were only interested in what had happened at the station and on the rig, not my subsequent adventures.

Afterwards, a Dr Foster (who'd never been anywhere near Gloucester, he told me) examined me and said that I'd been concussed and that they were keeping me in a couple of nights for observation.

I drifted in and out of sleep for the rest of the day and night and awoke the following day to the sound of church bells. After being fed and re-examined, I had my first visitor, David.

'How are you feeling?' he asked.

'Wishing I had a tenner for every time I heard that.'

He smiled faintly.

'Sorry, David. Aching, otherwise OK.'

'Good. When are they letting you out?'

'Tomorrow, I hope. They're checking me for concussion.' I suddenly remembered the station. 'What's been happening?'

'Well, we've been closed down. NII are on site, and will be until we've got it all sorted out.'

'Where were you on Friday, David? Kenny was trying to get you all—'

'I was at home,' he said tiredly. 'My phone was faulty. You know, sounds like it's ringing to the caller, but nothing at my end.'

'Bloody marvellous. When did they get you?'

'A police car came round about half an hour after the Scram.' He sighed. 'I couldn't believe it. Then we realized that you were missing.' He looked away. 'I thought you were dead.'

'David, what caused it?'

'The Scram? Oil,' he said. 'Crude bloody oil, fouling up the condensers. We've got Power Performance in now, trying to clean them up.'

'So it *was* sabotage . . .'

'You know that, and I know it, but how do we go about proving it?'

'But oil! How could that have got—'

'You've forgotten the oil terminal at Parrett. Suppose a ship discharged some in the bay and—'

'But oil floats. How would it get down to the intake?'

'What if it were heavy oil discharged at low tide?'

'Oh, come on! What about this?' I pointed to my head. 'I gather you picked up quite a few bumps on your adventures—'

'Not this one, mate. I was—'

'Michael, I believe you, I was just playing Devil's advocate. The Devil being WANT and all her works.'

'I suppose they're pretty happy?'

'Crowing. But there's worse than that.'

'Tell me.'

'After the Scram, I felt I had no choice but to tell Doll about Steve.'

'I suppose not. But surely, he's in the clear for—'

'He isn't, that's the problem. The police called at his in-laws, and it seems that Steve and Jane took themselves off again the day after they arrived—'

'Oh no.'

'Oh yes. And now nobody knows where they are. As you can imagine, I'm not exactly Doll's flavour of the . . .' He tailed off as the nurse approached.

'Inspector Doll is here,' she said to me. 'D'you feel up to answering some more questions?'

'Well, you can't fault his timing,' David murmured.

'All right,' I said to the nurse. 'I'd appreciate some more painkillers as well, though.'

She smiled and brought them to me, together with Doll. He watched me take them, then said, 'How are you feeling, Mr Hempstead?'

David and I exchanged grins.

'Fine,' I said, non-committally.

'Good. Now, there are a few points in the statement you made that I'd like to go over.' He read it out to me and I agreed that it was what I'd said.

'Let me get this clear,' he said. 'You were standing on the platform, looking down over the rail, when something made you turn. You saw a shadowy black figure, then you were struck.'

'Yes.'

'And you hadn't noticed a boat of any kind anywhere near the rig?'

'No.'

'I've been told that you may be suffering from concussion, which as you know, can play funny tricks with the memory. Is it possible that you slipped somehow, fell into the dinghy and knocked yourself out?'

'No.'

'Please, Mr Hempstead, think carefully.'

'I have thought. I was on a different side of the rig from where I'd tied the boat. Besides, what happened to the outboard motor and the oars?'

'Perhaps the outboard was dislodged when you fell.'

'Pretty unlikely, even if I did fall, which I didn't. And it doesn't explain where the oars went.'

He grunted and wrote all this down. 'You were unconscious for how long?'

'I don't know, but judging from the distance the tide took me, about four hours.'

'A long time. Whoever hit you made a good job of it.'

'A thorough job, Inspector.'

He smiled. 'A thorough job.' He leaned forward slightly. 'Could it have been Steve Holford?'

'I simply don't know. Although I wouldn't have thought so.'

'Why not?'

'From my knowledge of the man.'

'Even though, as we now discover, he tried to sabotage the power station a few days earlier?'

'D'you have any more news on him, Inspector?' David asked before I could reply.

'None,' Doll replied rather coolly. 'He and his wife have simply vanished.'

'That doesn't necessarily make him guilty of anything,' I said.

'No, but we simply don't know where else to look. And before you say WANT to me, Mr Rossily, it may interest you to know that we've questioned all the main organizers, and they can all account for that period of time. The same goes for the period in which Mr Broomfield died.'

I'd forgotten about Peter. 'Is there any more on that, Inspector?'

He paused. 'There is, as a matter of fact.' He waited. 'Neither the PM nor the forensic findings are entirely consistent with suicide. There is bruising to the body and face that may have been the result of a struggle, although it's difficult to be sure with half his head missing.'

'You mentioned forensic evidence.'

'Broken glass in the carpet. Not much, and very small pieces, since it had been swept up. But the depth in the carpet pile indicated that it had been broken very recently, perhaps during a struggle. And we found the remains of a whisky bottle in the rubbish bin.'

'That explains the smell when we got into the house,' I said to David.

'There was also some blood,' continued Doll. 'Only a small amount, but again very recent, and of a different group from Mr Broomfield's.'

'Not really conclusive, Inspector,' said David.

'No, sir, but enough to make us wonder.'

'There is something else, Inspector,' I said, and told him about Peter always calling his wife Patricia, never Pat.

'A shame you didn't mention this earlier, sir.'

'It only occurred to me after I saw you,' I said. 'And I have been somewhat occupied,' I added pointedly.

'Quite so, sir.' He turned to David. 'Would you agree with what Mr Hempstead has just said, Mr Rossily?'

'I do remember that he always called her Patricia, but I couldn't swear to how consistent it was.'

'Well, it further strengthens the case for foul play,' Doll observed when he'd written it down in the form of a statement. 'But it doesn't get us any nearer to who actually did it.'

After he'd gone, David said, 'I don't think he's really grasped yet that these deaths, and what happened to you, are part of the same thing.'

'Don't underestimate him. I think he understands more than he lets on.'

'For instance?'

'The way he questioned me about being clobbered and set adrift—'

'But all he did was to keep suggesting that you'd somehow done it yourself.'

'He was putting the alternatives. He didn't necessarily believe them, he just wanted to eliminate them in his own mind.'

'If you say so.' He paused, glancing at the earphones behind my head. 'Do those pick up local radio?'

'I think so. Why?'

'I may as well tell you. I'm going to be a radio star tonight.'

'Oh?'

'Orchard Radio, five minutes at the end of the six o' clock news. Me and E.T.'

'Who's E.T.?'

'Elizabeth Tregenna, who else?'

I smiled, then said, 'But why you, David? Why not Sir?'

'Sir was asked, but he nominated me to do it,' he said thoughtfully. 'Although not out of love for me, I'm sure.'

'He's trying to distance himself,' I said. 'Give the impression that the problems are your responsibility.'

'Possibly. I'm not particularly bothered, though.'

'David, listen to me. Don't underestimate Elizabeth Tregenna. She's clever, manipulative, and also very irritating, so for God's sake watch your temper.'

His head went back in a *Who, me?* gesture, then he said, 'Don't you worry, sunshine. You'll be listening, then?'

'I wouldn't miss it for the world.'

I had one more visitor that day. My heart gave a thump when the nurse asked me with a sly grin whether I felt up to seeing a young lady and it took all my will power not to look disappointed when Rhiannon came in. She likely guessed though. She's very perceptive.

'You look like Rambo with that bandage round your head,' she said as she sat down.

'Oh, thanks.'

'Any time.'

She didn't ask how I was feeling, so maybe David had said something to her. She produced a basket of fruit, which she put on the cabinet beside my bed.

'Not very original, I know, but I couldn't think of anything else.'

'Thanks, Rhiannon,' I said, meaning it. Then: 'Have you been busy?'

'Yes and no. Mostly I've been accompanying Miss Underwood round the station and answering her questions. She knows her stuff, doesn't she?'

'She certainly does. What about clearing up the oil?'

'Power Performance have nearly finished one of the condensers. John's in charge of cleaning the drum screens and ducts.'

'We might be running by next year, then.'

'Bitch. Although we do miss Don for this sort of thing. He did know how to organize people.'

'Yes.' I wondered how much she knew about the investi-
gation, but decided not to say anything. Instead I said,
'You've heard about David's elevation to celebrity status?'

'Yes. He'll be good, so long as he keeps his temper.'

'Exactly what I told him.'

We grinned at each other.

'How's that old diesel of yours coming along?' I asked.

'Nearly as good as new now. We're taking her up to
Lydeard tomorrow for the tests I told you about.'

We chatted companionably for another twenty minutes
or so and then she left.

Why is it we don't love those who love us? I wondered,
watching her go. There was a chain of us. John. Rhiannon.
Me. And Sarah.

The nurse showed me how to find Orchard Radio, and
after the six o' clock news, Liz and David were introduced.
Liz kicked off in the most devastating fashion.

'In the few weeks since we came here, there have been
three deaths associated with Desolation Point. There has
been a fatal accident and a suicide among the senior staff,
and a child has died of leukæmia, which we contend was
caused by radiation. There has also been a leakage of radioactive material into the sea, the very thing we were assured
could not happen in this country. And now there has been
an emergency shut-down, a Scram, I believe it's called,
apparently because of some oil discharged by a ship . . .'

I tried to imagine David's feelings as he listened to all
this.

'We in WANT accept the need for power generation, of
course,' Liz concluded, 'but there are *better* and *safer* ways of
doing it . . .' It suddenly occurred to me that she sometimes
sounded a bit like Maggie Thatcher.

'With respect, Ms Tregenna,' David began, his voice
uncharacteristically mild, 'you are speaking of these matters as though they are established facts, and they are
not—'

'Are you trying to say that these deaths haven't occurred, that radioactive material did not escape, or that there has been no emergency shut-down?'

'No, I am not saying that. I am saying that the *causes* for them have not yet been established, although current medical opinion is that there is no connection between nuclear power and childhood leukæmia . . .' He then went on to deal succinctly with the other matters she'd raised.

'France produces seventy per cent of its electricity by nuclear power,' he said. 'If we in Britain don't move at least some way in the same direction, in twenty years' time, we'll be dependent on the French for half our electricity, and still not have satisfied the environmentalists.'

'You say that,' Liz countered, 'but it's not as though Desolation Point is even reliable, is it? It'll be at least a month before you're producing electricity again.'

'Oh, I think you'll find we'll be generating electricity before then. This week, I have every reason to believe.'

I hope you're right, I thought.

'For the sake of the public,' Liz said, 'I hope you're wrong.'

'There's nothing amiss at Somerset Nuclear Electric,' David said. 'It has been our . . . misfortune that problems have arisen at a time when the ladies of WANT have been able to manipulate them.'

This was a mistake and Liz was on to it in a flash:

'Do I understand you to mean that if we hadn't been here, your problems, as you call them, would not have come to light . . . ?'

Four/three to David, I thought when it was finished. Although Liz's emotional opening speech may have counted for more. Evens, perhaps.

The next morning, Dr Foster examined me and said I could go home.

'What it boils down to,' he said, deadpan, 'is that we need your bed.'

'Oh.'

'Seriously, Mr Hempstead, take it easy for a few days. Concussion's a funny thing and can have unpleasant sequelæ if you're not careful.'

Then my various wounds were rebound by the nurse and I was discharged. David came to take me home.

'Well, you're certainly looking better,' he said when we were in the car. 'When are you coming back to work? Tomorrow?'

'I'm not sure,' I began, 'I'll see—'

'I was joking, you idiot.' He started the car and eased it out of the park. 'Well, how was I?'

'Pretty good, on the whole. Shame about that slip at the end.'

'Yeah. I knew it was wrong as I was saying it, but it was too late by then.'

'Are you really going to start up this week?'

'B circuit, tomorrow.'

'You're kidding.'

He glanced at the clock on the dash. It was nearly one.

'We pulled up the rods and went critical an hour ago. We'll synchronize and start generating electricity at midday tomorrow.'

'But that's fantastic. How did you manage it so quickly?'

'Power Performance sorted out the condensers, and John did an excellent job on the rest. Maybe the responsibility's good for him.'

'Why the hurry?'

'I'm trying to show NII what a good team we have.' He found a cigarette and pushed in the electric lighter in the dash. 'If I can demonstrate what a dedicated team of workers can do *despite* the best efforts of pressure groups to embarrass us, then I think we'll have scored a coup.'

'It'd be a coup de grâce if anything went wrong,' I said

before I could stop myself. Then, 'I take it you've got Sir's approval?'

'Yes, although he's not happy.' He glanced quickly at me. 'I'll be honest with you, Michael, I think my job's on the line.'

'But why——?'

'If I can make this work, it'll undo some of the damage WANT's done.' He drew on his cigarette. 'Can't you see, Michael? The government are wavering now about Nuclear Power. If WANT get away with it with us, then give one or two other nuclear stations the same treatment, it could just tip the scales the wrong way.'

'I think you might be overstating it. I hope you are.'

'No. What I've just told you's the good news. The bad is that the oil in the condensers has been analysed and it's the same chemical make-up as a load recently delivered to Parrett.'

'I simply can't understand that,' I said.

'I simply don't believe it. Unfortunately, to the ignorant, it looks like yet another loophole in our system.'

We talked around the problem until we got back to the cottage.

It smelt damp as we walked in and seemed to be saying, Oh, you're back, are you?

'It smells a bit damp in here,' David said. 'Ever thought of having it damp-proofed?'

'It was done about two years ago,' I replied patiently. 'By your brother-in-law.'

'Oh. Well, these old cottages always smell a bit damp, don't they?'

He hovered and fidgeted.

'Would you like a coffee?'

'No, I'd better be getting back. Make sure we're still on target.'

'Midday, you said?'

'That's right.'

'I might come in for that.'

'Are you sure? I thought you were supposed to rest for a few days.'

'Just while you synchronize.'

I didn't do much for the rest of the afternoon. The pain in my head came back, bringing with it an overwhelming lethargy.

Also, I was feeling a bit sorry for myself. I'd hoped Sarah would have made some effort to get in touch with me, if not come and seen me.

Perhaps she doesn't know, I thought hopefully, toying with the idea of going to look for her.

But I lacked both the energy and the nerve.

In the evening, Rhiannon and John called. They'd brought my car over, which was decent of them. They stayed for coffee and pleasantries and seemed very much together. I wasn't fooled, though. After they'd gone, I went to bed.

CHAPTER 19

I slept for ten dream-filled hours and when I woke the worst of the pain seemed to have gone, although the muzziness was still there. Something important was flitting round my head, but I couldn't trap it.

Got up, made breakfast, moped about. Decided I would go in, to see if Sarah was there, if nothing else.

Had a bath, found some fresh clothes and at eleven-thirty, drove to the station.

My heart revved painfully as I approached the gate. She was there. I pulled up beside her.

'Michael, you look terrible, what's happened to you?'

'I'll tell you later. I want to see you, Sarah.'

'All right.' She stepped back. I eased the car to the gate . . .

''Morning, Mr Hempstead.'

'Hello, Ron.' I felt for my pass but couldn't find it. Or my keys. *They must have been taken on Friday . . .*

'Ron, has anyone said anything to you about my keys?'

'Your keys? No, sir. Why d'you—?'

'Have the cameras been installed on the lower gate yet?'

'Tomorrow, sir. Why d'you ask?'

But my brain had gone into computer mode. What a coup it would be for WANT if something went wrong now . . .

But would they know about the restart today?

They'd know. So what would they . . . ?

The release of radiation.

The reactors?

No—too dangerous—they'd go for something like . . .

Me and Sarah by the Cooling Ponds Pump House . . .

Sarah: '*I can't understand why this is accessible from the outside. Isn't that a security hazard?*'

Me: '*Not unless some lunatic, who also happened to have the right card-key, broke in and put a bomb on one of the pumps . . .*'

'Why d'you ask, sir?' Ron said again, cutting through my thoughts.

'Ron, my keys were stolen on Friday night and I think someone's used them to put a bomb in the station.'

He gazed back at me without expression. 'Where, sir?'

'Cooling Ponds Pump House, but . . .'

He turned away. 'I'll get bomb disposal to check.'

'Ron!' I jumped out of the car and caught his shoulder. 'Ron, I think it'll be timed for just after they synchronize . . .'

He looked at me for just an instant, then dived into the guard room.

'Bill, Bill!' He snapped instructions at him, then came running out with a couple of torches. He yanked open the passenger door and jumped in. I let out the clutch and put my foot down.

The nearest I could get to it was the executive car park. I switched off and followed him across the grass.

Ron found his card-key and thrust it into the slot. 'What is it exactly we're looking for, sir?'

'A bomb—I don't know any more than that.'

Another noise intruded—the whine of a turbine starting up, followed by a ragged cheer. I looked at my watch. Twelve.

Ron had the door open. I followed him in.

'Now, sir, where?' he said urgently.

'On one of the four pump systems, probably on the outlet side. You take those two, I'll take these—Ron—' I grabbed his arm—'is it generally known that the start-up was to be at twelve?'

'Let's just get on with it, shall we, sir?'

I nodded and ran over to the other pumps. Glanced at my watch again. Two minutes past.

Swallowed. Started searching the maze of pipework with the torch.

So much of it. So many shadows.

Next pump. Glanced at my watch—six minutes past.

Couldn't see anything. Must be here somewhere, or was it all my imagination . . . ?

'Mr Hempstead!'

Ron. I leapt up and ran over to him. He was pointing to a pipe at the back . . . and a small silvery object taped to it. If you didn't know, it could have been part of the pipework.

'Hold the torch, Ron, while I—'

'No, sir. My job, I think. Light, please.'

His knife was already out, he reached through the pipework and cut away the tape.

'Careful, Ron, it might—'

'No, this'll be gelly . . .' He pulled it clear and stood up—

'Just chuck it out on the grass, Ron, let the bomb disposal—'

'No, sir, we've fucked-up enough lately—it's going in the sea.'

By now, we were outside.

'Ron—'

'If you want to be useful, open the gate for me.' He tossed me his keys.

I ran as hard as I could for the gate. He followed.

'Michael! What's going on?' John Burton.

'Keep away!' I yelled. 'It's a bomb!'

The seaward gate. I shoved the card in, yanked it open and Ron shot past me, past the tamarisks, up the steps in the sea-wall.

'Throw it!' I yelled.

But I could hear him going down the other side . . .

Then there was a crack, no louder than a pistol shot.

I tried to get to the sea-wall, but my legs were so heavy and I . . .

A face swam into view—Fitzpatrick, shining a light into my eye.

'How are you feeling?' he asked. Then, 'What's so damn funny?'

'Nothing. Nothing's funny.'

He grunted. 'I understand you've been concussed?'

'I was hit over the head two days ago and they said I was concussed.'

'They being?'

'Northhead Hospital. They discharged me yesterday.'

Another grunt. 'Well, they ought to know what they're about.' He put the spotlight away. 'I can't find anything else wrong with you. Go home now, and rest. Take these.'

He gave me some pills and told me to call my GP if I had any more symptoms, then got up to go.

'Doctor?'

'Well?'

'The man with the bomb, Ron . . . ?'

He hesitated.

'He's dead, Mr Hempstead.' Doll's voice. 'That makes three. I need to ask you—'

'He's going home,' snapped Fitzpatrick.

'This really is very important, sir.'

'Oh, very well. Five minutes.'

I gave him the barest facts before John Burton drove me home in the Midget.

John and I had never really got on and it hadn't been made any better by the fact that he saw me as an obstacle to his designs on Rhiannon, but that afternoon he treated me like a brother. He insisted on putting me to bed and if I hadn't told him to bugger off, I think he'd have got in with me. I fell asleep almost immediately.

I got up and had something to eat in the evening. Someone must have picked John up, because the Midget was still there.

David phoned me early the next morning.

'Is one allowed to inquire as to your health?'

'Better, thanks.'

'Good. Good.' Then: 'I owe you one, Michael.'

'That's all right. Any developments?'

'Several, actually. That's why I'm phoning.'

'Well, get on with it.'

'The police have taken in all the leading lights of WANT for questioning. Not before time.'

'Which leading lights?'

'Long Liz and her fancy man, and our friend Katriona Litchfield.' He couldn't keep the glee out of his voice. 'Two or three others, including, I'm sorry to say, your girlfriend.'

'You don't sound very sorry,' I said.

'I'm sorry for you, sunshine, but the police had no choice.'

There was no point in arguing. 'What about Steve?'

'There's no sign of him, or Jane. The police are still looking.'

I let out a groan. 'I hope to God he isn't involved.'

'You and me both. I shall be in deep shit if he is.'

'You said several developments.'

'Indeed I did. The Counter-Terrorist people have become involved. They want to speak to you.'

'I'm not allowed out. Doctor's orders.'

'Don't you worry, when they're through here, they're on their way round to you. I'll give them directions.'

'Thanks, *sunshine*.'

They arrived later in the morning, two of them. One of them was tall and lean with a military moustache, a film producer's ideal of what a Counter-Terrorist should look like. He was called Brigg. The other was smaller and more intense and called Stanway. Commander and Inspector respectively.

They accepted the offer of coffee, expressed sincere wishes for my speedy recovery and generally made themselves pleasant. And carefully studied me all the while.

'We've become involved, Mr Hempstead—' This was Brigg, who did most of the talking—'as I'm sure you realize, because of yesterday's bomb. However, that was almost certainly connected with the attack on you four days ago, and possibly with the deaths of Waterford and Broomfield and the contamination of the station's cooling system.' He didn't have to consult any notes, I noticed.

So far, so good.

They took me through the attack on the rig, just picking up on the odd point. The problems came with the bombing.

'There are a couple of things I'm not quite clear about.' Brigg again, while Stanway studied me. 'First, what made you realize that a bomb had been planted?'

'I didn't know for sure, I just suspected.'

'What made you suspect?'

'As I told you just now, it was the fact that my keys were missing and knowing that the start-up—'

'You hadn't noticed their absence before, when you got home from hospital and tried to open your door, for instance?'

'My house keys are on a separate ring.'

'I see. So you realized that the person or persons who attacked you might well have your work keys. How did you get from there to a bomb?'

'As I said earlier, in the circumstances, it was the next logical step.'

'Why didn't you contact the police, the emergency services?'

'Because I only realized all this when I arrived at the station, by which time, it was too late.'

'And yet, when you arrived, you managed not only to work out that there was a bomb, but where it would be.'

'That wasn't so brilliant, as I explained earlier. They couldn't plausibly go for another accident, so they decided to compromise security, preferably with the release of radiation. To me, that meant a bomb around the Cooling Ponds.'

'You've mentioned *they*. Who are *they*?'

'Well, WANT. Who else?'

'What about Steve Holford?'

I hesitated. 'If Steve is involved, it'll be because WANT put him up to it. I take it you still haven't located him?'

'No. And Ms Tregenna emphatically denies putting him up to anything.'

I shrugged. 'She would, wouldn't she?'

'Possibly, but I'd like to look at the problem from a different angle for a moment. I still find it difficult to understand how you knew *exactly* where the bomb would be.'

'I didn't know *exactly*, it took us nearly ten minutes to
find the bloody—'

'It would have taken longer, too long, if you hadn't speci-
fied the Pump House.'

My head had started aching again and I'd had enough.
'What is this?' I demanded. 'Are you trying to say I planted
it? Because—'

'No, we are not,' interrupted Brigg. 'We don't think that
at all. What we're wondering is whether somehow, inadver-
tently, you passed the information of where to plant the
bomb to somebody.'

Their eyes seemed to probe my head.

'I don't see how,' I said as easily as I could, thinking:
Uncanny how they home in to the right spot. 'It's not the
sort of thing we blab about.'

'I'm not suggesting that you blab about anything. But
you may have got carried away by your enthusiasm for
your work. Or by the company you were with, perhaps.'

I looked back at them, not replying.

After a silence, Brigg said, 'You escorted Ms Sarah
Brierly around the station on two occasions. On the second,
you showed her the Cooling Ponds.'

'Yes.'

'Could you have let the information slip then?'

'I could have, but I didn't.'

'Mr Hempstead, please, we're not accusing you of anything, we're just asking you to think very carefully about
what you may have said.'

Head buzzing furiously, I adopted the position of Rodin's
thinker for a moment, then: 'No, I can't actually recall
saying: If you ever want to sabotage this place, remember
to put your bomb *there*.'

They glanced at each other again before Brigg said, 'I'm
sorry you should choose to regard this matter facetiously,
especially since a man was killed. Shall we try again?'

'All right, I apologize. It was in bad taste.'

'Imagine you're back at the Cooling Ponds with Ms Brierly. What are you talking about?'

'Er—she was trying to make out that the Cooling Ponds were intrinsically dangerous because of the radiation in them, and I was trying to persuade her otherwise.'

'All right,' said Brigg. He leaned forward. 'Did you at any time mention or point out to her the Cooling Ponds Pump House.'

I said firmly, 'Not so far as I remember.' My first outright lie.

Brigg said, 'All right, Mr Hempstead, we'll leave it for the moment. Let's turn to the two previous deaths.'

We then went over the killings of Don and Peter while Stanway took notes. I was half expecting them to return suddenly to the previous subject to try and catch me out, but they didn't. They did, however, tell me as they left that they'd want to speak to me again.

After they'd gone, I collapsed on to the sofa, utterly drained, lacking the energy even to find some painkillers.

I'm not by nature a liar. I'd never told a lie of that magnitude before.

So why had I done it? If Sarah herself was innocent, which I was sure she was, where was the harm in telling the truth?

Maybe she'd somehow let slip what I'd let slip to her.

Or was David right and she'd played me for a sucker from the start?

CHAPTER 20

At first I thought it was Brigg come back with the rubber hoses but when I opened the door, it was to find Sarah.

'Hello, Michael. Can I come in?'

I stood aside, then closed the door and followed her into the living-room.

'How are you feeling?' she asked.

'Shitty.'

'I'm sorry.' I didn't say anything, and after a pause, she said, 'Michael, I need your help.' Still I didn't speak. She continued, 'Liz and the others are still being held by the police. They didn't have anything to do with what's happened, and I'm sure that if you and I go over everything together, you'll see that, and be able to help us.'

'No,' I said. 'I'm not going to help you.' My head was throbbing and I was very fed up. 'I've been beaten up and set adrift in the Bristol Channel, and the station has been sabotaged three times now, last night with a bomb. I was with the man who was killed. He was an ordinary bloke, wife, two kids—'

'I know and I'm very sorry, but it wasn't us.'

'Who else could it have been? Who else has anything to gain?'

'I don't know, but it wasn't us. Maybe it was someone trying to discredit us.'

'That's sick as well as ridiculous.'

'No more than to suggest that we could do it. Michael, we are non-violent, we are not bombers.'

'No?' I took a step towards her. 'You listen for a minute. That bomb was in just the place where I told you a bomb would release radiactivity. And when did I tell you? After you'd chatted me up for a second visit to the station. You've played me for a sucker from the start.'

'I have not,' she began angrily.

'You know how I got this?' I pointed to my Rambo band. 'I was hit over the head just half an hour after I left you at the Queen's Head, then I was dumped in a dinghy in the channel—'

'Michael, I know nothing about that, you have my word, nor do I—'

'Your word is worthless. You told me you knew nothing about Katriona Litchfield and the stuff she was writing.'

'I *didn't*—'

'You pretended you couldn't understand why Liz was being so provocative at the party when she was trying to take my mind off Kat—' I broke off and stared at her. 'And then you opened your legs for me.'

She stepped forward and gave me a clout that knocked me off my feet on to the sofa. My head spun . . .

'I'm sorry, but you asked for that, Michael.'

'You'd better go,' I said with difficulty, my voice faraway.

She stood there indecisively. 'Are you all right?'

'No,' I mumbled, 'I'm not. But your particular style of non-violence only makes me feel worse . . .' I swallowed.

'D'you want me to call a doctor?'

'Tablets beside my bed.'

I heard her running up the stairs and a few moments later she was back with the tablets and a glass of water. I swallowed three of them.

'I lied to the police for you, you know,' I said.

'Don't talk. Lie back. I'll get you a cold flannel.'

'Don't want any more old flannel from you,' I mumbled as she put it on my head. It felt beautiful.

I must have dozed off, no idea how long. When I woke, she was still there.

'Are you feeling any better?'

'I think so, yes.'

'You worried the life out of me,' she said. 'You were so white.'

'And you thought that another death might not exactly help the cause just now.'

'No.'

We smiled, tentatively, both perhaps wondering whether any trust was possible.

'We'd better talk,' I said.

She nodded, lowering her head.

I said, 'Did you tell anyone what I said about the Pump House?'

'Yes,' she said, still not looking at me. 'Several people.'

'Who?'

Now she looked up. 'Can I tell you how it came about?' She continued without waiting for an answer. 'It was obvious you had a . . . you were keen on me, and when I told the others, they said I should encourage it in case I could learn anything useful. Skeletons in closets, I mean,' she added quickly. 'Scandal. I didn't want to, because of finding that body and because I didn't think it was fair on you. But I did, as you know.'

'So who did you tell about the Pump House?'

'I was—debriefed, if you like—by Liz, Jonathan and Anna. Katriona was there as well.'

'Anyone else?'

'N-no.'

'I wonder . . .' I broke off. 'Is it possible that Katriona is some sort of mole for another organization?'

'I doubt it. She and Liz are very close.'

'Perhaps she let the information out unintentionally to someone.'

'But who would stand to gain by bombing a power station?'

'I don't know. Anarchists? Environmental extremists of some kind?'

'Surely they'd have claimed responsibility by now.'

'Possibly. Let's get back to Katriona for a moment. You still don't know how she got the information for that first article she wrote?'

'Yes, I do as a matter of fact. It wasn't me. We have a member working inside the station.'

'Who?'

'I can't tell you.'

'Sarah, for God's sake—'

'I can't tell you because I don't know.'

I let out a sigh. 'All right. Why did you ask me round to Liz's house that evening?'

'She wanted to meet you.'

'Why?'

'I—I'm not sure. To sound you out, I think.'

'All right. But why did Katriona come round that evening? Didn't she know I'd be there?'

'No. It was a mistake. She just dropped in.'

I looked at her, thinking. 'I have to ask you this, Sarah. I know why Liz went for me after that, but why did you let me . . .'

'Have sex with me? Because I was overwhelmed, I suppose.'

'What do you mean, over—'

'What do you think I mean? The moon, the sea, the night air. The scent of that tree. You. You'll have to make of it what you can.'

'I was overwhelmed too, Sarah.'

'Yes, but it's all right for you, isn't it? You're a man, you're allowed to be overwhelmed, women aren't. Aren't supposed to *open their legs*.'

'I apologize for saying that,' I said quietly. 'I didn't know what to think. Men don't like being used, either.'

She was silent, looking down at her hands.

I continued, 'I'm glad you were overwhelmed.'

She said, still looking at her hands, 'The same applies to the next day. I came here because I wanted to.' Now, she looked up. 'I was half hoping you'd come back to the Queen's Head that night, but you didn't.'

'No. I was lying in a dinghy in the middle of the Bristol Channel.'

'How did that happen, Michael?'

I told her as much as I could remember.

She shivered when I got to the end.

'I'd have died. D'you think it was the Exmoor Beast?'

'I don't know.'

She said, 'So you think you interrupted someone pouring oil down the water inlet?'

'I must have. That's when the temperatures and flow-rates went haywire.'

'And you didn't recognize who hit you?'

'I just have this vague memory of a figure in black. I'd assumed it was a wetsuit.'

'You know we can all account for where we were at the time?'

'So I was told, but I didn't for a moment think that that could be any of you.'

'Don't be quite so sure. There aren't many things that Liz couldn't do if she tried.'

I smiled at her perversity. 'But I take it you don't think she did this?'

'I don't think, I know. Liz could no more harm another human being than a sheep start eating meat.'

I must have looked sceptical because she said, 'You don't still think any of us could have had anything to do with any of this, do you?' She got to her feet. 'Michael, if I mean anything to you at all, come with me now and talk to Liz, please.'

'How were you intending to take me there?'

She had the grace to look embarrassed. 'I was hoping, in your car.'

'I'm really not up to driving at the moment.'

'That's all right, I'll drive. Please, Michael. We must get this straight in our minds.'

'I'm sorry, but I don't see what good it'll do.'

She let out a sigh. 'Oh well. I suppose I can't really blame you. Can I borrow your phone, please? To call a taxi.'

I smiled wryly. 'It's all right. We'll go in my car.'

'I have to go to Lydeard first, to pick up some documents for her.'

'All right.'

It was getting dark by now, so we put the hood up. She drove expertly.

'I used to drive a lot,' she said when I told her. After a pause, she continued, 'You said something about having covered up for me with the police?'

'They knew I'd shown you over the station and they asked me the direct question: had I shown you where to put the bomb, even in innocent conversation? I said no, which was a direct lie.'

'Did they press you?'

'They most certainly did. I thought it was them again when you arrived.'

'Well, I am grateful, although it wasn't necessary.'

She concentrated on her driving for the rest of the journey. As we drew up by the cottage, she said, 'Look, there's a light on. They must have been released.'

She got out and walked quickly up the path. I followed. She knocked on the door.

Silence.

She knocked again and called through the letter flap, 'Liz, it's me, Sarah.'

Then there were footsteps and the door was opened.

'Hello, Anna,' said Sarah, surprised.

'Hello, Sarah. We came down as soon as we heard. To see if we could help.'

'Oh, you've spoken to Liz, then.'

'Yes, on the phone.'

There was a pause, then Sarah said, 'We've come to pick up some documents she wanted, actually.'

'Oh. Well, feel free.'

As I followed Sarah inside, Tony came into the room.

'Hello there,' he greeted us.

'Sarah's come to fetch some documents for Liz,' said Anna.

'Oh, right.'

'What have you done to your hand?' asked Sarah.

'Oh, an argument with a milk bottle,' he said, holding up his right hand. It was heavily bandaged.

'Nasty.'

'You should see the milk bottle,' he quipped. Then he continued, 'It wasn't much, but I managed to get it infected afterwards. You look as though you've been in the wars too, Michael.'

'Argument with a metal rod,' I said. 'The rod definitely came off better. In fact,' I continued, turning to Sarah, 'I'm not feeling so good, so d'you think we could find what you need and go, please?'

'OK, sure. Won't be long,' she said to the others.

She led me down the stone-flagged hall and unlocked a door that led into a small office. She pulled open a cupboard and sorted through the papers inside, picking some out and putting them to one side. Beside her, I fidgeted with impatience.

'Michael,' she said, 'is there something wrong?'

Yes, desperately wrong—'No. Except that I really do feel rough. Can we go, please?'

'I'm sorry. Of course.' She closed the cupboard, picked up the papers and re-locked the office as we went out.

'Found what you were looking for?' asked Tony as we got back to the kitchen.

'Yes, thanks,' said Sarah. 'We're just off.'

'Stay and have a coffee. Anna's just percolated it.'

Sarah looked at me.

I said, 'If you don't mind, I'd really rather not.'

'But we do mind, don't we, Anna?' He laughed. 'Seriously, do have a coffee. It'll make you feel better.' He pulled out a chair.

'Oh, all right. A quick one.'

We sat down. There was silence, except for the tinkle of hot coffee into the cups as Anna poured.

Sarah said, 'D'you think Liz and the others will be released soon?'

'I'm surprised they haven't been already,' said Tony as Anna handed out the coffee. 'There's no real evidence against them. What do your people feel about things, Michael?'

'Pretty sick,' I said, adding more milk to my coffee to cool it down. 'And angry. I know I am. But having spoken with Sarah, I don't believe that your lot are responsible any more.'

'Well, that's something,' said Sarah.

'So who do you think is behind it?' said Tony.

'I've absolutely no idea. Some anarchist group?'

He pursed his lips and slowly shook his head. I drank more coffee.

Tony said, 'How did you bang your head, Michael? In that dinghy of yours?'

'No. It was at work.'

'It's just that from the position on your head, it looks as though the boom caught you by surprise.'

'I suppose it does,' I said. I finished my coffee. 'Shall we go?' I said to Sarah. 'I really am feeling rough.'

'OK, let me just finish this.' She took another mouthful. 'You've reminded me,' she said, 'talking about boats. Is yours still in St Katherine's, Tony?'

'Yes. Why?'

'Well, I saw one just like it the other day when I was at Watchport with Michael. Even had a similar name. *Marlin*, isn't it?'

In the silence that followed I stared down at my empty coffee cup, pretending I hadn't heard.

Tony's chair rattled on the stone floor as he pushed it back and stood up.

'It's no use, Michael,' he said. 'You're not that stupid.'

I looked up. He held an automatic in his good hand. Anna stood up too.

Sarah gazed at him in complete astonishment and said in a choking voice, 'It *was* your boat. It was *you!*'

CHAPTER 21

'B-but how?' Sarah was saying in bewilderment. 'You were in London when the oil got into . . .'

'Anna was in London. I was in the Bristol Channel, with Michael here.'

Curious, I thought, looking at his face. He looks exactly the same as he did before, here and at my cottage, and yet now, he's got to kill us . . .

'You could have just chucked me into the sea, Tony.'

'I wish I had now.'

My headache was quite gone, my mind concentrated wonderfully.

'Why didn't you?'

He gave a short laugh. 'I didn't think it was necessary. A mistake I shan't make again.'

Anna had got up. Sarah and I were still sitting, Sarah nearest him.

I said, 'How long have you had this planned?'

He looked at me for a moment as though considering whether to answer.

'I suppose it goes back to when Liz first started WANT, although it didn't become practicable until WANT had moved down here. You see, Don Waterford was by way of being a cousin of mine, removed a couple of times. Anyway, I knew him well enough to know that he both despised and disliked his boss and had no loyalty to Somerset Nuclear Electric. In other words, he was ripe for corruption. I don't know why I'm telling you this.'

His gun was in his left hand. I was sure he was right-handed.

'I'd like to know,' I said. 'Really. To know how close I

was.' Anna was behind us, watching . . . But if I could get to his gun before he could react . . .

A smile touched his lips. 'I can believe that.' Pause. 'Well, both the radiation leak and the oil were Don's ideas, but he couldn't get hold of any radioactive material in a suitable form without Peter Broomfield's help, so he enlisted him.'

'I hadn't realized Peter was actually part of it.'

'Oh yes, a vital part, although not a very willing one. But he was short of money and under Don's influence.'

Which explained his misery after Don had been killed.

'Why did you kill them?' I asked, shifting slightly as I spoke.

'I didn't, not Don anyway.' He sighed. 'Unfortunately, Peter didn't believe me. When I went round to his house to pay him off, I found him drunk and with a shotgun. He said he knew I'd killed Don and nothing I said could persuade him otherwise. I managed to get the shotgun off him, but then he went for me with the broken whisky bottle and cut my hand before I could overpower him.' He gave another short laugh. 'The cut didn't bother me until I got it infected, probably in the sea.'

'What about Liz?' said Sarah in a small voice. 'And Jonathan?'

'They weren't involved.'

'So who put the radiation in the Drum Screen Pit?' I asked, moving again a little to face him. 'Don was already dead, so I suppose it must have been Peter . . .'

'No, it wasn't. They packed radioactive sludge in a shell made of gelatine, or something similar, then Don dropped it in the pit, where it took a couple of days to dissolve.'

'Don was nothing if not ingenious,' I said, shifting again. 'Why was he so keen to be the one to show Sarah around the station?' The trouble was, with Sarah in the way, it was going to be difficult to reach him quickly enough.

'Because we'd intended Anna to be the representative. Liz decided on Sarah at the last minute.'

'How did you manage the oil? You left no traces on the rig.'

'Don again. He knew someone at Parrett and arranged the oil, for a fee. I towed it behind my boat in a plastic submersible, ten tons of it.'

'But why didn't I see your boat when I went out to the rig?'

Tony chuckled briefly. 'You would have, had it been there. We'd towed the submersible out a few days earlier and secured it to the rig below the waterline at low tide. Don showed me how. All I had to do that evening was to swim out and expel the oil with compressed air, then release the submersible to be carried away by the tide.'

He sighed again. 'It took longer to blow out than I'd thought, and had already started to take effect in the station before I was ready to release the submersible. And that *had* to be released so that sabotage couldn't be proved. Then you came out to the rig and I had to get rid of you before I could release it. It was as buoyant as a cork by this time.'

Which explained the out of focus shadow I'd seen on the screen.

'Then why the bomb?' I asked. 'You went to such efforts to hide the fact that the radiation and oil were sabotage, but a bomb could never be anything else.'

My legs were now free of the table and I was directly facing him.

'You're right,' he admitted. 'It was a gamble that didn't come off. I already had the device, which had been designed so that it wouldn't be noticeable on casual inspection. When Liz heard from our mole on Monday that you were planning to restart the reactor the next day, I thought the opportunity too good to miss, especially after what your boss had said on the radio. Firstly, it would make a joke of your security, which you were supposed to have tightened, and secondly, nothing gets Joe Public going more than the escape of radiation, whatever the cause. There would have been a Public Inquiry at the very least. But you managed to screw that up for us, didn't you, Michael. How did you know?'

I smiled and rearranged my legs slightly. 'When I realized my keys were missing, I remembered telling Sarah about the vulnerability of the Pump House.' I shrugged. 'The rest was intuition, I suppose. I read your mind, even although at the time I still thought WANT was behind it.' I looked up into his face. 'So why are you here now?'

'Tony, he's just wasting time.' Anna's voice was as brittle as ice. 'Let's get it over with.'

He held up a bunch of keys, my keys.

'I thought it might help things along if these and a few other items could be found here by the police when they get round to searching the place.'

'Tony!' Anna again.

'Yes, I'm afraid we have run out of time now.'

'Tony?' Sarah. '*Why?*'

He looked at her contemptuously. 'That's something you will have to work out for yourself, my dear—'

Faster than a cat, she jumped at him, taking us all completely by surprise. She caught his gun in both her hands . . .

As I lunged forward, he tried to punch her in the face, but his bandaged hand couldn't make a proper fist . . .

She held on. I reached him, caught his wrist. I knew Anna was behind me but thought I could get the gun first. I might have, had she not hit me over the head with something very hard.

CHAPTER 22

I was like sand, dissociated. Faraway voices.

Sarah: *He's dead, you've killed him.*

Tony: *Is he dead, Anna?*

Anna: *Yes . . . Oh my God, Tony, what are we going to do?*

Am I dead? I wondered.

Tony: *Leave him. We'll take her to the boat . . .*

Silence.

Then my heart gave such a thump I thought it would burst . . . I felt myself heave in a shuddering breath, then another and gradually, I came back together again. (Fitzpatrick told me later I'd been briefly in a state of *Apnœa*, or cessation of breathing, brought on by the concussion.)

I turned over and pushed myself up. My head swam. They were taking her to the boat, to Watchport . . . Police . . . find a phone . . .

I looked around but couldn't see one, then remembered the office . . . Staggered down to it. Locked.

Ineffectually threw my weight against the door, sobbing with frustration.

Have to find a phone-box . . .

Rhiannon's house . . .

Stumbled out of the door and down the path. The Midget was gone . . . Why?

The fresh air helped me to think better. Because it would look as though Sarah had killed me, driven my car to Watchport, *where she'd be found drowned in the sea . . .*

Rhiannon's house . . .

Then I remembered the old bikes in the lean-to . . .

The tyres were soft and there were no lights and I thought as I pedalled: How ironic if I'm stopped by a village bobby on my way to phone 999 . . .

Rhiannon's house was only a quarter of mile away, but when I got there it was in darkness. Have to look for a phone-box . . .

Then I heard the rumble of a big engine and re-membered: She was testing her diesel at Lydeard station.

On the bike again, legs like feeble springs, then I was freewheeling down the track to the station yard. I could see the loco against the station lights, a cloud of blue smoke hanging above it. Pedalled over, jumped off and climbed the steps to the cab, banging with my palm on the door. It opened.

'Michael! What on earth's the matter?'

I took a deep breath and told her in a couple of sentences —them, rather; John Burton's head was peering over her shoulder.

'Where's the phone? I must get the police.'

'Over there, in the station. Michael, wait. How long since they left?'

'Ten minutes, I don't—'

'They've only got to get to Watchport from here, but the police'll have to get there from Northhead . . .'

'Where's the phone . . . ?'

She said, 'We could get there before them . . . John, you go and phone—what's the name of the boat, Michael?'

'Er—*Marlin*.'

'The owners?'

'Tony and Anna Linden. They're driving a black Porsche. They've got my Midget as well.'

John jumped down and ran for the station.

'Try and clear a path for us,' Rhiannon shouted after him and he raised a hand in acknowledgement.

'Up, Michael, quick.'

I scrambled up and she slammed the door and took her seat. Incredibly, the smell took me back for an instant to the last time we'd been in the cab together, then there was a click as she pushed the power-handle to the first notch and an answering clunk from the contacter behind us as the hydraulic drive engaged.

It was as she released the brake and the big loco lumbered forward that the lunacy of what she was doing hit me.

'Rhiannon, we'll never make it, I should've—'

'No?'

The wheels screeched as we crossed the points from the siding. She opened the handle another notch and the exhaust echoed as we went under a bridge.

'Watchport's eleven miles by rail,' she said, 'nearly thirteen by car. And we won't have any hold-ups.'

She pushed the power-handle wider and the engine's grumble became a roar as the hydraulic drive bit, and I felt the seat press into my back. Foliage began streaming past. The time between the rail joints shortened. The twin rails gleamed in the headlamps and the sleepers flickered beneath us. I glanced at the speedometer. Fifty.

'He's got a Porsche,' I said. 'He'll be doing seventy.'

'Not tonight he won't, not on that road.'

As though to endorse her, we flew over the main road and a line of slowly moving traffic. 'It's the county fair. And then they've got to get out to their boat.'

And then Anna'll have to get back to the Porsche, I thought. They can't leave that there as well as my car.

Sixty. The exhaust boomed as we went under another bridge and for the first time I wondered if we really might do it . . .

Click-clack . . . The loco swayed as we hit a bend and Rhiannon eased back the power, then opened it again. Another bridge, buildings loomed and a platform shot past—

'Crowhurst,' she said. 'Downhill from now on.' She pushed the handle up another notch. Sixty-five. Then braked as we lurched round another bend.

A light ahead, flashing.

'Level-crossing,' she said. 'Automatic.'

The bells jangled harshly as we swept past. She opened the power-handle wide and we surged forward . . . sixty . . . sixty-five . . . seventy . . .

Another level-crossing, a car waiting, bells howling . . . I couldn't see more than a hundred yards ahead . . .

'You're going too fast,' I shouted, clutching her arm.

'Get off, you stupid—' She pushed me away. 'Stop being a back seat driver. The track's reasonably straight till we get to Stogford.'

I peered ahead, swallowed. Another level-crossing flashed by, then a bridge. Then we hit a bend and the loco pitched, throwing me into her . . .

'All right, all right!' she snapped as she pulled back and hit the brakes. The loco squealed and shuddered as we shot another bridge and went through Stogford station.

Then came a series of bends and she juggled with power and brakes to keep the speed as high as she could before opening up on another straight.

I glanced at my watch and saw to my astonishment that we'd only been moving for eleven minutes. We went over the main road again, the traffic was as heavy as ever and I began to believe we'd do it—although I had no idea what I'd do when we got there . . .

'Oh, bloody hell!' Rhiannon.

'What—? Oh, *shit!*'

A gated level-crossing, shut.

Rhiannon hit the brakes. 'You'd better—'

'Keep going!' I shouted.

A second's hesitation and she opened up again, gave a blast on the horn as a car bumped over the rails in front of us . . . Then the gates were flung aside as we smashed through, the second pair grinding along the sides of the loco.

Willcombe station.

'We've lost our lights,' I said.

'It doesn't matter, we're nearly there.'

I peered through the screen, trying to make out what was ahead.

'Isn't Doniton halt here somewhere?'

She pulled back on the handle and braked violently; the engine swung, hit the side of a platform, then we were past . . .

The sea, gleaming on the right.

'Half a mile,' she said. 'Where d'you want me to stop?'

I shut my eyes for a moment. 'If we're ahead of them, beside the esplanade. I'll find their tender and sink it . . .'

'What if they're already there?'

'I don't know. Beside the docks . . .'

We slid into a deep cutting, the sides throwing back the noise of the engine, then we emerged beside the docks. At first I thought we'd beaten them, then I saw the Porsche on the esplanade.

'Stop!'

A tortured scream from the brakes. I opened the cab door and jumped, tumbled on the rough grass. Picked myself up, ran back a little way, then clambered over the fence, snagging my trousers on the barbed wire.

The docks were brilliantly lit, throwing light into the harbour. A tender was beside a big blue cruiser. A man, Tony, was climbing aboard.

I looked around. No one had seen me. A ship was loading at the far jetty. I ran through the parked lorry trailers, past a darkened ship, towards the far jetty. A crane was lowering heavy crates into the forward hold.

I stopped, glanced at the launch. Twin plumes of smoke went up as the engines started. On the esplanade, the Porsche pulled away. I began running again.

I don't know what I intended to do, jump on from the end of the jetty as he went through the harbour mouth, I suppose . . .

I heard Tony open the throttles as I reached the crane

. . . don't remember thinking anything . . . looked up to see Al Williams at the controls. He hadn't seen me, but a shout told me someone else had.

I jumped on to the crane, into the cab.

'Michael, what the fu—?'

'Sorry, Al.' I pushed him off his seat and he fell to the ground. Which lever? *Which lever?*

My hand went out, touched one, there was a whine as the crane arm swung slowly round, taking the crates with it. They contained car parts, I noticed . . .

The launch was at the harbour mouth now. I saw Tony's face through the glass as he looked up at the swinging crates . . . The engines roared as he opened them. Al's hand was on my arm, pulling . . .

I punched the release button and, very slowly, the crates dropped, smashing into the launch, obliterating the cockpit . . . The boat skewed, drove into the harbour wall.

I kicked Al away, jumped, sprinted to the end of the jetty. Below me, the launch wallowed in the swell. The engines screamed as the props came out of the water, then suddenly cut. I jumped, landed in the well at the stern . . .

A door at the bottom of the well. I ran down, kicked it open—a grinding as a wave lifted the boat against the harbour wall—the cabin was half filled with water . . . Sarah lay tied on a bunk, eyes open and terrified.

I splashed through the water, caught her under the shoulders, hauled her to the door, slowly, slowly up the steps . . .

Men crowded the end of the jetty. Rhiannon. She threw me a lifebelt. I slid over the side, pulling Sarah with me, and grabbed the belt. Police on the other jetty. One threw a rope, I splashed through the water towards it. Another lifebelt was thrown.

One of the police shouted to me, 'Anyone else on board?'

I nodded, lacking the energy to shout.

He pulled off his jacket and leapt, landing in the stern of the sinking boat.

I found the rope and the other policeman was pulling us round the wall to a ladder . . .

CHAPTER 23

Three days later I was released from hospital and the day after that Doll called on me at home and brought me up to date.

Anna had been arrested on arrival at her London home. She'd denied everything and even called her solicitor, until they told her that Tony was dead, killed when the crates hit the boat, and that Sarah and I were still alive. Then she'd broken down and admitted the conspiracy.

'Now that the shock's worn off a bit,' Doll said, 'self-interest has come into play, i.e., she was an unwilling partner, dominated by her husband. No killing was ever planned and she'd been quite horrified when she discovered he'd killed Broomfield.'

'What about Don Waterford?' I asked.

Doll took a breath. 'She categorically denies that. She says: Why should her husband have killed him?'

'To keep him quiet?'

Doll made a face and shook his head. 'Risky business, bumping off one's accomplices; the ones left alive tend to object. Witness Broomfield.'

'So what do you think happened?'

'I was hoping you might have some idea.' He met my eye. 'Sir.'

I shook my head. 'Tony Linden denied killing Don when Sarah and I found him at Liz Tregenna's place, but in the circumstances I didn't believe him. Are you sure he didn't do it?'

'No, not absolutely. But as Mrs Linden says, why should he have done?'

'What about money? To avoid paying him off.'

'The Lindens stood to make a fortune out of this. Millions. Paying Waterford was peanuts.'

I sat up. 'How d'you mean, Inspector? Fortune out of what?'

'You didn't know?'

I shook my head.'

'Linden headed a syndicate that holds a massive shareholding in McGarrick's, the firm that's building the gas-fired power stations. If nuclear power were phased out, the shares would double in value.'

I slumped back, stunned by the simplicity of it.

'Well, it certainly explains a lot.' I looked up at him. 'Did you ever find the submersible he used to transport the oil?'

'Yes. It was washed up at Dorlock a few days ago.'

'Have you found out how he got hold of the oil?'

'A friend of Waterford's at the oil terminal. We shall be pressing charges. Mr Hempstead,' he continued before I could say any more, 'we seem to be drifting away from the subject of who killed Mr Waterford.'

'I'm sorry, but I can't help you there. I've no idea.'

'Perhaps we should go back to looking for those in the power station who had reason to dislike him.'

'We did that before, if you remember, and it didn't get us anywhere.'

'No, it didn't, did it, sir. But perhaps you'd like to give it some more thought now,' he continued stolidly, 'and let me know if you think of anything.'

I assured him I would and saw him off the premises. At the door I said, 'What about WANT's mole inside the station?'

'We still don't know—for sure. Mrs Tregenna won't tell us, and since it's not vital to the case, we can't make her. Thinking about it, though, I'd watch your receptionist, Sharon Phillips, if I were you.'

*

The next morning I was on a fast train to London.

After we'd been hauled out of Watchport harbour, Sarah had been treated for shock and the following day had gone to stay with her parents, who also lived in Streatham. I'd spoken to her twice on the phone, but she'd been detached and non-committal, so I'd decided on some affirmative action. I wasn't supposed to drive at all, but I'd had to drive as far as the mainline station.

I found her parents' house quickly enough (a smart town house with steps leading up to a white-painted door) and rang the bell. The door was opened by a well-dressed, middle-aged lady with a pleasant face. A little girl with curly fair hair clung to her and peered up at me.

'Mr Hempstead?' The turbanlike dressing on my head probably identified me. 'Do come in. We can't thank you enough for what you did for Sarah. I'm sure she'll be pleased to see you.'

I suppose she was. Pleased, but not overjoyed. After a chaste kiss and the ritual of tea and pleasantries, I was left alone with her.

'I still find it all so hard to believe,' she said with a shudder. 'Not so much what happened, but the fact that it was Tony and Anna. I've known them for so long . . .'

When I told her what Doll had told me about Anna's denial that Tony had killed Don, a thoughtful look came over her face. 'I do remember that evening,' she said. 'It was the day before you took me round the station the first time. We were all at Liz's house in Lydeard and Tony and Anna had just come down.' She looked up at me. 'When was it that Don was supposed to have been killed?'

'Between eight and nine.'

She nodded. 'I thought so. They arrived at six, maybe a little longer. We all had a meal and then Tony ran me over to the Queen's Head. He suggested we have a drink and we ended up having quite a long chat.' She gave a wry smile. 'As you observed yourself, he could be good company. But the point is, he couldn't have killed Don, he was with me.'

'What time did he leave?'

'Nine, nine-thirty?'

'Could it have been Anna?'

She shook her head. 'She was at Lydeard and Tony had the car. Besides which, I don't think she was capable of killing. Conniving at killing, perhaps, but not a planned killing.'

I said slowly, 'I wonder if it could have been Peter after all . . .'

'But Peter accused Tony of it, that's why Tony killed Peter.'

'We've only Tony's word for that.'

'And Anna's. And why would he deny one killing when he so casually admitted the other?'

'I don't know,' I said. 'It rather looks as though we're left with a mystery.'

'Yes,' said Sarah. A shadow crossed her face. 'And one that I don't want to talk about any more. Or think about. In fact, Michael—' she looked directly at me—'I want to forget about everything and everyone connected with Desolation Point.'

There was a small silence. Then I said, 'I don't blame you. So long as it doesn't include me.'

She looked away. 'No,' she said carefully, 'it doesn't include you. In that I'll always remember you with fondness and gratitude.'

I went over to her and knelt (yes, on one knee) and took her hand. It was slack in mine.

'More than remember me, Sarah, please. We'd be making a mistake if we gave up on each other. We're right for each other, I know it.'

She smiled sadly. 'How can you say that? What Tony and Anna did was indefensible, and I mean before they started killing people, but I still believe in WANT's aims and I'll go on working for them.'

'But—'

'Michael, I believe that what you do for a living is morally obscene.'

'But that's not me. It's my job, not *me*. Can't we look at each other as people . . . ?'

She slowly shook her head. 'It wouldn't work.'

'All right then, I'll give up my job. I'm a qualified engineer, I can find another job.'

'Michael, why must you make this so difficult for me?'

She tried to pull her hand away but I stopped her. 'Because I love you. Because we're right for each other.'

'We are not. I'm sorry, but you leave me no option. I don't love you. I never could love you. We are not right for each other.'

'But that evening when we were at my house . . .' I cast round desperately for something to say. 'Can't we go on seeing each other, as friends?'

'No, Michael.'

'But, Sarah, I saved you . . . from Tony . . .' As I said it, I knew how wrong I was and the look she gave me was more damning than any words could have been.

There was nothing more to say. I got to my feet.

'Goodbye, Sarah. I hope you find what you're looking for.'

'Goodbye, Michael.'

I made my excuses to her mother (But won't you stay for lunch? No, I must be going, really. Oh. Well, thank you again, Mr Hempstead . . .) and left.

Some time the next day, I stopped thinking about her, because my brain simply wouldn't take any more. After a while I found myself thinking about Don instead, and just before five I drove over to the power station and went up to David's office.

'Michael, what are you doing here?'
I shut the door.
'It was you, wasn't it.'
'What was me?'
'You killed Don.'
He gazed at me. 'Are you out of your mind?'
'No. It has to be you. It wasn't either of the Lindens, or
any the rest of WANT.'
'How can you possibly say that?'
'How would they get in?'
'Well, Linden managed.'
'How would they get in *without my key*?'
'I don't know, but—'
'David, they all have alibis. Everyone who matters here
at the station has an alibi, except you and me. Rhiannon
and John were together. It wasn't me. And you were here.
On your own, after Sir left.'
He looked at me thoughtfully. 'Have you told the police
any of this?'
'Not yet.'
'But you will?'
'If I have to. David, if you give yourself up, you'll almost
certainly get away with manslaughter.'
'He was hit several times, remember.'
'Yes. Beside the Drum Screen Pit. You must have caught
him in the act of dropping that capsule in there. He attacked
you and you killed him—in self-defence.'
He smiled thinly. 'I may have caught him in the act of
dropping that capsule, but that wasn't necessarily why I
killed him.'
'I'm giving you a way out.'
'Don't you want to hear the truth?'
'Not particularly.'
'You're going to hear it anyway.' He stood up. 'He was
blackmailing me.'
I let out a breath. 'It figures. A woman?'

'Yes. And as you know, not the first. I don't think Helen
would have forgiven me again. And I do love her, and my
kids.'

'You can still say you caught Don sabotaging the station
and in the ensuing fight—'

'I wouldn't have to say anything, if you didn't. Michael,
Don was a waste of space. Do you mourn him? Don't you
think he deserved it?'

'No, and yes. But that's—'

'So why d'you have to say anything?'

'I've been asking myself that all day. Apart from the fact
that Doll suspects *me* of it, I can't unsay what I've just said.
I'd always be a potential threat to you, imagined or real,
a threat that one day you may wish to eliminate. We neither
of us can live with that.'

He turned and went over to the side window. 'I suppose
not,' he said at last, quietly. He turned back to me, this
time holding the shining piston paperweight.

I said, 'I wasn't fool enough to come here without telling
someone first.'

'Letter to your bank manager? To be opened in the event
of my death?'

I shook my head. 'I told Rhiannon.'

'Rhiannon?'

'That's right.'

'What did she say?'

'She was surprised, naturally. She agreed with me that
it probably was self-defence, when you caught him contami-
nating the cooling water.'

He laughed softly. 'I think I'd have guessed you were
lying even if I hadn't known.'

'No, David. Rhiannon and I—'

'You see, Michael, it was Rhiannon that Don caught me
with.'

I gaped foolishly.

'Yes, I thought that would surprise you. You didn't think

she'd consort with anyone else so long as you were around, did you.'

'I—I didn't think about it.'

'No,' he agreed. 'Probably not. Oh, she's still in love with you, but she has her needs, too. And you did use her.'

'How long's it been going on?' My eyes flicked round the room, wondering if I could get to the door ahead of him.

'Oh, about six weeks. And there's no one left on this floor,' he said, reading my mind, 'they've all gone home. No one else will hear you above the noise.'

He was right, and I wouldn't make it to the door.

'Doll's not a fool,' I said. 'He smells a rat anyway. Another death and he'll be on to you.'

'No, Michael, on to *you*.'

'Oh, rubb—'

'This time, I will make it to the Seal Pit. Suicide, bought on by remorse from killing Don.'

He lunged at me. I dodged round his desk, picked up his ashtray and flung it at him. It flew past his ear, showering him with cigarette ash. He put his hands under the side of his desk and heaved, upturning it on to me. I jumped back, tripped over the waste-paper bin and fell on to my back. He was round the desk and on to me in a flash. I kicked, caught his knee. He lashed with the piston, caught my instep, fell on top of me as I creased with the pain . . . He raised the piston. I clung to his wrist . . .

He was overpowering me, even the forfeit of my life couldn't give me enough strength . . . He tore his hand away, raised the piston again . . .

Then his body went slack and he collapsed beside me.

'I can't do it.' He tossed the piston away and took out his cigarettes.

'Why not?' I croaked. 'If you could kill Don?'

'Oh, Don was different. He deserved to die.' He lit his fag and blew smoke. 'Besides, it *was* manslaughter in a way.' His eyes squinted round at me. 'Want to hear the truth? The whole truth?'

I nodded.

'He was up here in my office after work that day, demanding a rise. Oh, not in blackmail terms this time, he ordered me to put him in for a special discretionary bonus and, d'you know, that made me even madder than the money he was taking from me. Can you understand that?'

'Yes, I can.' I could, too.

'And the fact was, he knew it.' He looked up at me. 'The money wasn't the reason he was doing it. He'd always loathed me, because I was his boss, and not the other way round. If it had been you, he'd have loathed you.'

I nodded and said, 'Yes, probably.'

'He was doing it to . . . get back at me for existing.' His tongue touched his lips. 'So I agreed, although why the words didn't choke me there and then I'll never know. You see, he'd have carried out his threat to tell Helen. That would have given him as much pleasure as the money.'

I could see that too.

'After he'd gone, I had to go and see Sir, as you know. More vile sherry and equally vile pleasantries. Then I came back here. I was thinking about Rhiannon—and you—as a matter of fact. She's a nice person, d'you know that?'

'Yes, I know it.'

'You should have shown it. Anyway—' he lit another cigarette from the stump of the old—'a bit before eight I saw the bastard strolling around down there in the dusk. I saw him from that window. You can see the Seal Pit from there as well and I thought: That's where you're going, sunshine.

'I put the piston in my pocket and went down, but when I got there, he'd disappeared. And d'you know, I was glad. Glad I wouldn't be able to kill him. Then I saw a movement by the Drum Screen Pits and realized it was him. Believe me, Michael, I knew at that moment I couldn't do it. Then

I noticed how furtively he was acting and as I watched, I saw him drop something in. I went up quietly behind him and asked him what the hell he was doing. He jumped out of his skin, but when he saw it was me, he laughed.

'What's it to you, *sunshine*?' he said. Then he said, 'Come to think of it, *sunshine*, there's no reason why I shouldn't tell you, is there?' He came up to me and said, 'It's a favour for a lady, or at least, a woman. Quite a lot of women, if you get my drift. Anyway, *sunshine*, you'll find out, to-morrow some time.'

'Suddenly, it was easy. I told him to go ahead and show my wife his dirty pictures, that I wasn't going to connive at sabotage. And he believed me. For a moment it was marvellous watching his face change. Then, he went for me. I should have realized he would.

'He was stronger than me. He had his hands round my throat and I was trying to pull them away—then I re-membered that.' He pointed to the piston. 'I got it out of my pocket and hit him round the head with it, again and again.

'At first, it didn't seem to make any difference, then sud-denly, he collapsed on me . . . and d'you know Michael, I felt *glad*, glad this time because I *had* killed him.'

'No,' I said. 'You felt glad because it was he that was dead rather than you. Not because you'd killed him. There's all the difference in the world.' Sarah would have been proud of me. 'Why didn't you put him in the Seal Pit?' I asked.

'It was just as Doll said. I heard a security guard, panicked and dropped him in the Drum Screen Pit. Then I went straight to my car, logged out, and went home. The next day I decided to leave things as they were, and the day after, when we had the radiation scare, I thought I could pin it on to that. And now, I need a drink.'

He got to his feet and made for the cabinet.

'No, David.' I struggled up after him.

'Why the bloody hell not?'

'Because we're going to sit here, sober, and work out the best possible story for Doll.'

Doll told me later he'd known it had to be either David or me.

The story we concocted was that David had suspected that Don was up to something, had watched him, then accosted him by the Drum Screen Pit after he'd seen him drop something in. Don had attacked him and David had killed him in self-defence, then panicked when he'd heard the security guard coming.

But how had he known that Don was dead? the prosecutor wanted to know.

Because he'd tried to bring him round and failed. (And the PM had shown that Don was dead before he went into the water.)

Why had he been carrying the piston?

He was taking it home as a present for his son.

Why hadn't he taken the opportunity to confess after the 'radiation leak'?

He should have, he could see that now. But at the time he'd felt caught up in a web of lies from which he couldn't escape . . .

The jury believed him and he was acquitted of murder, although found guilty of obstructing the police. For this he was sentenced to one year's imprisonment, suspended for a year.

Sir wanted to sack him, but the directors, after protracted heart-searching, overruled him because David had done what he'd done in defence of the station. (And, probably, they were afraid of the bad publicity.) So he was kept on, although his position is still precarious. It's certainly put a stop to his womanizing, and his relationship with Helen seems to have improved. (I asked her one night about the WANT leaflets at their house. Apparently, some children at Megan's school had given them to her to give to her dad. For a 'joke'. She'd put them in the lumber room, meaning to dispose of them later.)

Steve and Jane Holford had surfaced (fortunately *after* the Lindens' role had been established) from the hotel in the Forest of Dean where they'd gone to escape the in-laws.

WANT dropped the legal action against Somerset Nuclear Electric and then disbanded, but I hear that Liz Tregenna has bought some land in Cornwall and started a wind farm.

The best news of all is that Steve is back at work and Jane is pregnant again.

Rhiannon?

She's too proud to say so, but she still loves me, and part of me's glad about it. I know she's ten times more . . . worthy than Sarah, but I haven't been able to get Sarah out of my system yet . . .

David says I need my head seeing to. He's right.